That Weekend in Paris

That Weekend in Paris

Inglath Cooper

Contents

Copyright 1

Books by Inglath Cooper 3

Map of Paris 5

Dillon 6

Dillon 14

Klein 24

Dillon 29

Josh 35

Dillon 41

Dillon 45

Dillon 57

Dillon 63

Klein 72

Dillon   77

Dillon   84

Riley   90

Klein   98

Klein   109

Dillon   114

Riley   123

Dillon   132

Klein   137

Dillon   145

Klein   157

Klein   162

Josh   170

Dillon   175

Dillon   183

Klein   192

Dillon   205

Klein   212

Dillon   221

Klein   230

Dillon	*233*
Dillon	*238*
Klein	*247*
Riley	*251*
Dillon	*254*
Klein	*261*
Dillon	*264*
Klein	*269*
Dillon	*273*
Riley	*276*
Klein	*279*
Dillon	*285*
Josh	*287*
Dillon	*290*
Klein	*298*
Riley	*304*
Klein	*309*
Dillon	*314*
Klein	*320*
Dillon	*323*

Epilogue   327

If You Enjoyed That Weekend in Paris. . .   329

That Birthday in Barbados   331

Books by Inglath Cooper   333

Dear Reader: 335

About Inglath Cooper   336

Get in Touch With Inglath Cooper   338

Copyright

For permission requests, write to the publisher at the email address below.

Fence Free Entertainment, LLC
Fence.free.entertainment.llc@gmail.com

Books by Inglath Cooper

That Weekend in Paris
That Birthday in Barbados
That Month in Tuscany
Swerve
The Heart That Breaks
My Italian Lover
Fences – Book Three – Smith Mountain Lake Series
Dragonfly Summer – Book Two – Smith Mountain
Lake Series
Blue Wide Sky – Book One – Smith Mountain Lake
Series
And Then You Loved Me
Down a Country Road
Good Guys Love Dogs
Truths and Roses
Nashville – Book Ten – Not Without You
Nashville – Book Nine – You, Me and a Palm Tree
Nashville – Book Eight – R U Serious

Nashville – Book Seven – Commit
Nashville – Book Six – Sweet Tea and Me
Nashville – Book Five – Amazed
Nashville – Book Four – Pleasure in the Rain
Nashville – Book Three – What We Feel
Nashville – Book Two – Hammer and a Song
Nashville – Book One – Ready to Reach
A Gift of Grace
RITA® Award Winner John Riley's Girl
A Woman With Secrets
Unfinished Business
A Woman Like Annie
The Lost Daughter of Pigeon Hollow
A Year and a Day

Map of Paris

Dillon

"Don't spend time beating on a wall, hoping to transform
it into a door."
—Coco Chanel

STAND BY YOUR MAN.

The title from the country song my mama used to play in our Smith Mountain Lake kitchen on Saturday mornings pings through my head, Tammy Wynette's gold-standard Nashville voice attached to the melody. She had loved her classic country, and no one hit the notes for Mama like Tammy.

But the song in my head scratches to a sudden halt, as if the needle's been dragged across the record. My eyes fly open.

Most of the passengers around me in the first-class cabin of the Air France flight are sleeping, blankets tucked up around their shoulders, eye masks in place.

I glance at my watch, see that we have three hours to go before landing in Paris.

I close my eyes again, remembering how many times I tried to talk Josh into taking a second honeymoon to Paris. Tried to convince him it was the perfect city for two people in love.

I guess he finally believed me. That it was the perfect city for two people in love anyway. The kicker? I wasn't the person he was in love with. Or the person he wanted to take to Paris. No, he'd opted for a newer, undamaged model instead of me.

Exhaustion tugs at me. I wish I could sleep like the people around me. I envy the fact that they will arrive relatively refreshed. But I hear Mama's voice again, clear as if she were sitting on the seat beside me. *Men mess up, honey. It's just a fact of life. What are you gonna do?*

Leave his ass. That's what I did. My subconscious offers up the response, and I already know what Mama's going to say.

Did you give him two arms to cling to?

No. I gave him a stiletto in the kneecap.

I hear Mama's indulgent laugh. *Not saying he didn't deserve that.*

Yeah, but it didn't fix anything.

Sometimes, forgiveness is the only thing that will.

I don't have it in me to forgive him.

Yes, you do.

No. I don't.

I raised you to have a forgiving heart, Dilly.

That was before sexting, and iCloud, and a husband too arrogant to remember he shared an account with you.

You shouldn't have been poking through his messages.

I wasn't poking. Okay, I was. But I had cause.

And who did you end up hurting the most?

Me, I guess.

Right.

You're the one who taught me to listen to my gut.

Yes, but did your gut tell you something was wrong in the marriage long before you found those messages?

Maybe.

Diillllly?

Yes. *Yes.*

I also taught you not to ignore things that need your attention.

That was the problem though. He hadn't wanted my attention. Not for a long time. I'd tested my theory with enough bait from the Neiman Marcus lingerie department to be sure of my conclusion. Hard to deny stone-cold not interested.

A collage of shots flip through my mind, each one set against the backdrop of the bedroom I'd shared with my husband. I watch myself in one scanty getup after another try to reignite my husband's attraction to me.

Staring out the window of the plane, I see the indulgent patience on his face, as if he is trying very hard not to glance at his watch or pick up the phone on the nightstand by the bed. I realize now there was probably a text message from her hiding behind the screensaver photo that still featured a picture of Josh and me accepting my songwriter of the year award.

I linger on that for a moment. Remember that night and how incredible it had been to reach a milestone I never imagined I'd reach.

To his credit, Josh had always believed I would.

From the moment I'd brazenly walked through the front door of Top Dog Publishing in Nashville and asked if I could personally hand my CD of original songs to Josh Cummings, he'd said I had what it took. Guts and talent. Not sure I ever agreed with him. But then desperation can look like guts when it comes to taking a risk.

As for the talent, I'd been writing songs since I was seven, picking out tunes on the pink guitar Mama gave me for Christmas. She had also believed in me, and it was her love for country music that fostered my own. Her voice behind many of the lyrics that flowed through my pen to the yellow notepad I still write on.

My phone dings with a text message that comes through the plane's Wi-Fi.

I glance at the screen. My stomach drops at the all-caps message blaring back at me. I tap in, read it fully.

WHAT THE HELL ARE YOU DOING, DILLON? THE TRIP TO PARIS WAS IMPORTANT BUSINESS FOR THE COMPANY. I COULD BRING CHARGES AGAINST YOU FOR FALSIFYING THE CANCELLATION OF MY TICKET.

I roll my eyes and shake my head. As far as I know, there's no law against canceling an airline ticket.

I'VE JUST SEEN THE CHARGE ON THE AMEX FOR A TICKET TO PARIS. I REPEAT. WHAT THE HELL ARE YOU DOING?

I consider this question. I suppose Josh deserves an honest answer, even though he did precipitate my actions with his decision to put aside our marriage vows. I'm pretty sure this isn't the time to point that out though. We can save that for the attorneys.

I tap into the reply box, hit the all-caps key, and start texting.

CONSIDER IT A SMALL PRICE TO PAY FOR MY WILLINGNESS TO GO ALONG WITH A NO-FAULT DIVORCE. ALL THAT MONEY I WASTED

ON A PRIVATE DETECTIVE, AND I DIDN'T EVEN USE THE PICTURES.

I can see that his response will be nearly instant because the little thingamajig indicating that he is typing rotates furiously as if it can't spit the message out fast enough. I can practically hear him fuming from across the ocean.

YOU'RE THE ONE WHO WANTED THE DIVORCE. WE COULD HAVE WORKED IT OUT.

I type an emphatic:

WHAT? A THREESOME?

YOU KNOW THAT'S NOT WHAT I MEANT.

IT WAS OVER THE DAY I STOPPED BEING ENOUGH FOR YOU. I GUESS, IN FACT, WHEN YOU DECIDED YOU NEEDED PERFECT.

AND NOW YOU'RE GOING TO TRY TO WRECK MY BUSINESS?

WHY WOULD I DO THAT?

WHAT ELSE WOULD YOU CALL CANCELING MY MEETING WITH KLEIN?

WHO SAID I WAS CANCELING IT? I HAVE EVERY INTENTION OF MEETING WITH HIM.

WHAT THE HELL ARE YOU PLAYING AT, DILLON?

IF YOU RECALL, HE WAS MY DISCOVERY.

WHAT DO YOU MEAN HE WAS YOUR DISCOVERY? IT'S MY COMPANY. IF I HADN'T AGREED TO SIGN HIM, HE WOULD BE NOTHING.

This is arrogant, even for Josh. We both know Klein could have been signed by just about any house in Nashville.

But then Josh's arrogance has been pointed out to me many times. In the early days, when I was starstruck with a head full of the flattery of his belief in me, I preferred to see it as confidence.

It did take confidence to build the kind of publishing empire Josh had built in Nashville. It didn't come easy. I should know that. And he'd started twenty years ago from the ground up with one writer.

So I would be the first in line to give him credit for the success he had achieved in a town where no one threw it at you without the substantial recognition you had something worthwhile.

But on this subject, the subject of Klein Matthews, he's wrong.

He *was* my discovery.

Dillon

"A good country song takes a page out of somebody's life
and puts it to music."

—Conway Twitty

Seven years ago

I OFTEN WENT TO the Bluebird Café for
inspiration, finding a quiet table in the back where I could
observe the singer-songwriters playing on any given
night. That was where I first heard him play.

He'd gotten in on a fluke, a cancellation at the last
minute by one of the well-known writers who'd had an
accident on the way to the round.

I would later learn that Klein had been new to Nashville,
and in the audience to absorb whatever he could to learn
about breaking into the business. The panicked manager
had approached me that night with a request to jump in
the round. And although I'd appreciated the request, I no
longer sang my songs in public.

And so, she'd put out a plea for a singer-songwriter in the audience willing to act as a stand-in. There were a few hands, but to her credit, the manager's gaze had fallen on Klein, where he'd been sitting near the back of the room. She walked straight over to his table, which happened to be only a couple away from mine, and said, "Are you up for this?"

He'd responded as if the opportunity were no big deal, when everyone around him knew differently. The Bluebird Café was well-known for bringing to light up-and-coming talent in Nashville. And the waiting list to play on a night like this was longer than long.

"You have any original songs?" she asked him, meeting his gaze with a clear understanding of what she was offering him.

"I do, ma'am," he said in a quiet, South Carolina drawl.

"All right, then. What's your name?"

"Klein Matthews."

"Well, Klein Matthews, someone else's misfortune has made this your lucky night. You got a guitar?"

"Yes, ma'am. In my truck."

"Best go on out and get it then. We're starting in less than five minutes."

He stood, unfolding a surprising height of six-three or better. I wasn't the only woman in the room whose gaze hung right there in a freeze-frame of awareness. He was stunningly good-looking, dark brown hair with a slight wave, longer at the front, shorter at the sides. He had an athlete's build, broad shoulders that tapered to a narrow waist, his black T-shirt stretched tight against a well-hinted-at six-pack. He wore faded jeans in the way they were meant to be worn, close-fitting, the legs tapering to a pair of worn biker boots.

He weaved his way through the tables and out the front door, a gaggle of admiring female gazes following him. I told myself the observation had nothing to do with anything other than the realization that he looked like a country music star, whether he already was one or not.

Josh wasn't with me that night. I do remember glancing at the wedding ring on my left hand. Since meeting Josh, I'd never had any reason to look at another man. I was as content being married as I had ever imagined being. Josh and I had a pretty great relationship, all things considered. It wasn't easy to combine marriage with work, but we'd somehow managed to do it.

Having said that, I don't know what made me look at my ring. Some ping of awareness I suppose my body must have recognized on a cellular level. I wasn't proud of it. Vows meant something to me. I had never taken them lightly.

But I do believe we have an innate ability to immediately recognize attraction when it presents itself. Acting on it, however, was another thing altogether. That was something I had never done.

Even so, from the first line of the first song Klein Matthews played during his turn in the round that night, I knew immediately I was witnessing the birth of a new star in Nashville.

His obvious gift was a rare thing. That combination of the ability to put words into a song that would move its listeners almost immediately. And a voice with the kind of delivery that made women want to go home with him after the show.

I turned on my phone recorder halfway through the first song, knowing I would send the recording to Josh as soon as Klein finished. I listened, rapt, lifted up and carried away by every word that gave me an instant visual into a small-town South Carolina life that no doubt had made him who he was.

The words to that song made me, like every other female in the audience, wish to be the girl in the back of that truck with him on a summer night. Before the last note of the song faded away, I had texted the recording to Josh. It wasn't five minutes later that he replied back, "Did he write that?"

I tapped back a quick, "Yes."

Two seconds later: "Sign him."

I took an empty seat at the table closest to the front to give me the advantage of speaking to him as soon as the round was over. I knew without a doubt, there were other scouts for competing houses and labels in the room that night. And that I would not be the only one wanting to sign Klein Matthews.

Almost two hours later, the round ended, and I quickly stood, weaving my way to the front. Out of the corner of my eye, I recognized my competition and their equal intent to reach him first. Anyone in the know would have found the scene a little ridiculous, all of us scurrying toward him as fast as we could without outright sprinting. But if I knew one thing, it was that opportunity didn't present itself very often. The ability not only to recognize it, but to act on it was what made the difference between winners and losers.

I made it to him first, sticking out my hand and saying, "Hi, Klein. That was amazing. *Truly* amazing. I'm Dillon Blake. Do you have a couple of minutes to talk?"

He raised an eyebrow, clearly surprised by my approach. "Hey. Yeah. I know who you are. You've written some amazing songs."

"Thank you," I said, a little taken aback by the recognition. But then I'd never gotten used to that part of it, people actually knowing my songs. "Do you think we could go outside where it's a little quieter?"

"Sure," he said.

Billy Sumner, an exec at Pinnacle Records, stepped up next to me and handed Klein a card. "Love to have a conversation with you, man," he said, ignoring me. "You got a minute?"

Klein glanced from me to Billy. Lucky for me, his polite, Southern manners took precedence. "The lady here asked for a few minutes, but I'm free after that."

"My number's on the card. Just give me a shout when y'all are done."

"Sure," Klein said.

Billy turned then and walked off, but not without first giving me a glare of disapproval. He wasn't used to being bested by anyone in this town, least of all someone who had previously rejected his advances.

"After you, ma'am," Klein said, waving a hand for me to lead the way through the still-crowded bar.

I walked with a deliberately measured pace, striving to appear less eager now that I had his attention. I'd learned from Josh that negotiating involved a skill set that wasn't natural to me. I wasn't very good at hiding my excitement when it came to discovering someone with talent.

In the parking lot, I came to a stop next to the black 911 I drove with equal appreciation and awareness that some part of it wasn't actually me. Josh had given it to me when I won songwriter of the year. I still felt more comfortable in the old Ford F-150 I'd driven into Nashville for the first time ten years ago. Still kept it parked in the garage. Still had it detailed once a month.

"Nice," Klein said, eyeing the car.

"Ah, thanks," I said, refusing the urge to apologize for the extravagance, another aspect of my past I still struggled with. It wasn't that long ago that I was still putting five dollars' worth of gas in my truck at a time and leaving my rent check at the landlord's door at 11:59 P.M. when it was due at midnight. "Well, that was truly incredible in there. How long have you been performing?"

He leaned against the side of the car, folding his arms across his chest. "Not that long, actually. I played baseball in college and actually got recruited to play for the Braves." He raised his right arm, bent at the elbow, and said, "Blew out my shoulder, and that changed all that."

"I'm sorry," I said.

He shrugged. "I figure there's a reason why I'm not supposed to be doing that. I've been writing songs for years but never dared to play any of them in front of a crowd."

"That would be why you haven't already been snatched up," I said, even as I realized I wasn't keeping my cards close to my chest.

Again, I'd surprised him. I realized he wasn't fully aware of his own talent. A better businessperson would have taken advantage of that insight. But I usually identified from the artist's point of view, and if I couldn't win him over with a fair offer, I didn't want to win him over.

He studied me with those intense eyes of his, as if he were trying to read my thoughts. I dropped my gaze, cleared my throat, and then looked at him directly. "My husband started Top Dog Publishing here in Nashville."

Recognition of the name flashed across his face, something like disappointment close behind it. "Some of my favorite writers are with Top Dog," he said. "You, of course, being one of them."

He named three other writers, and I realized he'd done his homework before coming to Nashville. "They're all great," I said. "We're lucky to have them."

"I never made the connection that you were married to—"

He broke off there, and I finished the sentence for him. "Josh. Josh Cummings."

"Yeah," he said. "I've read a good bit about him. He apparently has a gift for spotting talent."

"In all honesty," I said, "it's not that hard to spot the talent. But maybe a little more difficult to know when someone has all the ingredients."

"And what are those?" he asked, giving me a level look.

"A combination of things. A voice that stands out. Something to say. A vision of life that is both unique but layered with the things most people yearn for every day."

"What else?"

"A hunger to be heard. And the drive to follow through on it."

He considered what I'd said, glancing off past me for a moment at the front door of the Bluebird, where patrons were still streaming out at the end of the night. "You think I have those things?"

"The first three. The last one remains to be seen."

"Did your husband see those things in you?" he asked, surprising me.

"I think so. Except I never really wanted to be a performer."

"Why did you sign with him?"

"The answer might seem obvious, but we weren't actually dating when he signed me. I went with Top Dog because I did my research. I felt sure, based on the other writers who had signed with him, that was where I would have the most opportunity to get my songs in front of artists I would be thrilled to have record them. If you are looking to write and perform, I still think Top Dog will open the most doors for you in this town."

"I don't doubt that."

"How old are you, Klein? If you don't mind my asking."

"Twenty-three," he says lightly. "How old are you? If you don't mind my asking."

I'm surprised that he's turned the question to me, but maybe I needed this dousing of comparison to squelch the fire of awareness zinging around me. "Twenty-nine."

His gaze stayed centered on mine, and I could feel a dozen unspoken thoughts ignoring the obvious fact that he was barely out of college and I was married.

I reached inside my phone case, fumbling a bit, pulled out a card, and handed it to him. "If you'd like to talk further, give me a call, and I'll set something up with Josh.

Meanwhile, you should explore every option available to you, including meeting with Billy Sumner and anyone else who expresses interest in your work. I've found that's one way to make sure you don't have any regrets. To be honest, I'd love to sign you right now, but I don't really think that would be fair to you because you don't know what else is out there yet."

I walked around to the driver's side of the car, hit my remote key, and opened the door. I saw the surprise on his face and wondered for a moment if I had just done something incredibly stupid. Josh would almost certainly think so. But everything I'd just said to Klein Matthews was true. What was that old saying? If you love something, set it free. If it comes back, it was meant to be.

Maybe that applied to discovering talent as well. And as I pulled out of the Bluebird Café parking lot that night, glancing in the rearview mirror to see him standing exactly where I'd left him, watching me go, I had no way of knowing exactly how much of a crossroads in my life that night would end up being.

Klein

"We don't receive wisdom; we must discover it for ourselves after a journey that no one can take for us or spare us."
—**Marcel Proust**

WHEN YOU'VE GROWN up poor, it's not likely that you'll ever be completely comfortable with the kind of luxury found in places like the Ritz Paris hotel.

At least I don't think I'll ever be completely comfortable with it.

The South Carolina trailer park where I spent my years before foster care is about as far from the Ritz Paris as it is possible to be.

It's way past dinnertime when I let myself inside the hotel room with its king-size bed, now turned down for sleep, its thick, satiny sheets beckoning me as if they are a magnet for the fatigue that permeates my bones.

I'd landed in the city this morning, checking into the

hotel and then heading for rehearsals with the band. We'd skipped dinner, and I'm starving now, despite how much I just want to drop into bed and go to sleep. I grab a menu from the desk in the corner of the room, pick up the phone, and order a salad and a sandwich.

While I wait for the food, I head for the enormous bathroom with its gold fittings and walk-in shower. The label has definitely put me up in some beautiful places, but the opulence here is beyond anything I've stayed in before. This stay is courtesy of Josh Cummings, in return, I suppose, for the two number one songs I'd been lucky enough to chart this year. It was a very generous gesture, but I feel a little out of place staying here without the band.

When room service arrives, I answer the door in one of the hotel's heavy white robes. The waiter, an older man with gray hair and an air of style that seems to be innate to the French, greets me a pleasant good evening. He carries the tray into the room and sets it on the corner of the king-size bed. He keeps his eyes politely averted in the way of staff trained not to let on their awareness of celebrity guests. It still surprises me to be treated like someone famous, always makes me uneasy, as if someone's going to discover at some point that I'm actually an imposter. That my success has been a fluke.

I ask him how the weather is supposed to be tomorrow, and he proclaims it will be early spring perfection. And since I'll have most of the day free, I ask if he has any recommendations for nearby sightseeing. He immediately offers up, "The Louvre, of course. You can spend days viewing its treasures. But I recommend to pick your most intense interest and focus on that. You will not be disappointed. It is a most amazing place."

I thank him for the recommendation and hand him a tip.

"Merci beaucoup, monsieur," he says, and with a nod, leaves the room.

I sit down on the chair by the window with my food, tapping into the search engine on my phone and typing in "Louvre."

I spend a few minutes scanning the different areas of the museum, decide on the two things I most want to see: the Mona Lisa and the Venus de Milo.

The food is delicious, and once I'm finished, I sit back in the chair and scan through emails on my phone.

Most are work-related. But there's one from Riley. I consider scrolling past it, then tap in before giving myself a chance to change my mind.

"Hey. I know you're not reading my texts. Or I assume you're not because you're not answering. So here I am resorting to email. I'm sorry, Klein. I'm so sorry. I should have involved you in the decision. I just didn't think you were ready. Or that I was ready. You were touring. I tried so many times to make myself tell you. I wanted to. I really did. I just didn't want the two of us being together to be about anything other than you wanting to be with me. I didn't want you to come back to me out of some sense of obligation."

I stop reading there, clicking out of the mail app, and throwing my phone on the bed. I stand at the window, staring out at the Paris night. I feel as if a knife has been inserted straight through to the middle of my heart and is slowly being turned, the pain excruciating.

I keep thinking that time will make this feel better, bring me to the conclusion that she was right not to include me. But it's not a place I've been able to get to. There's just a gaping hole inside me, raw with grief and anger.

Was she right to question what my response would have been? Can I say for sure I would have done the right thing? Knowing I'd already decided the two of us weren't right for each other?

There's no law that says I had a right to know. A right to do anything other than go along with her wishes, whatever they were.

I just don't understand how that can be. How I could be fifty percent of what was needed to create that tiny life and not have any right whatsoever to be its father? Pictures play through my head, images of a baby boy or a baby girl. I squeeze my eyes shut, trying to turn them off. Tears leak down my cheeks, and I wipe them away with the back of my hand.

The minibar glares at me, beckoning me with assurance that it holds the key to turning off my thinking. I know I only have to open the door to find a row of small bottles that will provide temporary numbness, anyway.

The desire to give in to them yawns wide inside me. But that is a hole I do not want to jump into. Instead, I open the drawer in which I had thrown my running clothes, grab some shorts and a T-shirt. I throw them on, find my running shoes in the closet, and a couple of minutes later, take the stairs to the lobby and hit the cobblestone street outside the hotel at a pace certain to put my focus on the next breath and not the next thought.

Dillon

"When I dream of afterlife in heaven, the action always
takes place in the Paris Ritz."
—**Ernest Hemingway**

NEVER ONE TO skimp on luxury, Josh had made
a reservation at the Ritz Paris located in the 1st
arrondissement. I'd done some research on the hotel
during the flight over, not surprised that he had chosen
what was notably the most elegant hotel in the city, in
most of the world, in fact. I wonder if he would have taken
me here if he'd ever agreed to that second honeymoon.

The Mercedes taxi I've taken in from Charles de Gaulle
turns onto the enormous square that stretches out before
the architectural wonder that is the Ritz Paris. I'm
admittedly a little fascinated by its history and the fact that
it had been closed by its Egyptian billionaire owner for
a nearly four-year, $450 million renovation, the effects of
which are easy enough to see.

A black Rolls Royce sits at the entrance, the sportiest version I've ever seen, and I wonder if it belongs to the owner of the hotel, or if it is a perk for super notable guests. Just behind it is a black Range Rover, equally eye-catching. A driver stands by the back door, apparently waiting for his passenger.

I am welcomed by the dark-suited staff out front as if I am arriving royalty. I wonder if they have confused me with actual royalty who are booked to stay at the hotel. A Frenchman with beautifully accented English takes my bags, and another leads me to the front desk. I'm checked in by a lovely young woman with long dark hair and vivid blue eyes. Her French-accented English provides a distinct contrast to my Nashville-twanged responses, polite as I try to make them.

As she checks the computer screen, I glance around me at the elaborate lobby, its high ceilings and marble floors, the elevator that leads to the hotel's renowned spa. I feel alone for the first time since I'd left my car in the Nashville airport's long-term parking lot. Maybe it's something about checking into a hotel by yourself that does that. And maybe I'm a little intimidated by the luxury of this place and the realization that I would never choose it for myself because I would never think I deserved to stay somewhere reserved for the world's wealthiest people.

From first glance, the Ritz Paris is everything the reviews had raved it to be. It had first opened in 1898, and never once closed for over a hundred years. The current owner had apparently wanted it to remain the choice for the world's most affluent travelers and embarked on a renovation that ensured it would remain the destination for five-star luxury. Judging from the hustle and bustle of its extremely well-to-do clients this morning, it's clear he has succeeded.

"Ah, here we have it," the young woman whose name tag reads Céline says. "And it appears you've booked a suite. Excellent. You will be so happy there."

I'm tempted to ask her the rate, a little surprised Josh would have gone that elaborate in a hotel already so obviously expensive. But then he'd planned to bring her with him. The suite had been meant to impress his twenty-something girlfriend.

"We have your American Express on file, madame. Will that be sufficient, or would you like to provide me with another card?"

"The American Express is fine," I say.

She types for another minute or so and then hands me the key. "Henri will be escorting you to your room, madame."

She waves a hand toward an older gentleman standing at attention. He gives me a courteous smile, offers me a nod, and beckons me down marble steps to the rug-adorned marble floor and past the Bar Vendôme, which he points out as one of several beautiful places in the hotel to have a drink.

Farther down, he motions toward the hotel's Michelin award-winning restaurant where I could have breakfast, lunch, or dinner. As we continue along, he asks if I know of the hotel's history.

"A little," I say.

"You might know then that your American novelist Ernest Hemingway spent time here at the Ritz Paris. Our most well-known bar is named after him. It is an excellent spot to have a drink in the evenings."

"Thank you. I will have to try it."

We take an elevator to my floor, and the luggage arrives at the same time.

Henri points to the right and says, "After you." He takes the key from me and opens the door, waiting while I step inside. Since I'd taken an overnight flight, it's only a little after eight Thursday morning, French time.

A silver tray with a matching pot and a white porcelain cup sit on the table in the middle of the room.

"For you, madame," he says. "There's also a basket of buttered toast and jam. If you should like anything else from room service, please call that extension. We will be happy to bring it to you."

The coffee is a welcome sight. I wait while he pulls my suitcase from the cart and arranges it next to the luggage stand by the closet. He asks if there's anything else he can do for me. I tell him no and thank him, handing him a tip. He takes it without looking at it, nods once, and lets himself out of the room.

I take off my lightweight coat, drop it on the bed, and immediately pour myself a cup of the steaming coffee. The tray holds heavy cream and white sugar cubes. In a moment of indulgence, I add a bit of both, taking a sip and closing my eyes for a moment against the wonderfully robust flavor.

I carry the cup to the balcony, staring out the window at the magnificent city before me. Cars, taxis, and mopeds, horns honking, all vie for position on the street below. It's early June, and vibrantly colored flowers adorn the window boxes of the building across the street. The sky is a vivid blue today, the sun lending its light to a late spring day.

My thoughts veer back to the realization that Josh had intended this room and its incredible views to be for his girlfriend. I wait for the familiar stab of hurt that always accompanies reminders of his infidelity, but it isn't as sharp this morning. I wonder why. Is it because I've one-upped him by coming to Paris to meet with Klein? Righted the ship of justice a bit?

I'm human. So maybe.

But somehow I don't think that's it.

I try to remember the love I once felt for him. Try to

recall the sense of security I knew in never questioning what I thought we had.

It isn't there. In its place, there's just a hole of sadness where happiness had once been.

I want to put all the blame on him, but I've logged enough hours with the counselor I've been seeing to know I played some part in it, knowingly or not.

I turn from the window, stare at the enormous bed, and torture myself with a vision of Josh and his twenty-something making use of it.

I close my eyes hard and blink it away.

Enough.

I have a canvas of blank hours before me. The show is tonight. Until now, I haven't thought about what I would do for the duration of the day. The thought of sleeping for a few hours tugs at me with an irresistible pull, but the desire to see the city has more appeal. I decide on a quick shower, a change of clothes, and a walk on the streets of Paris. I pour another cup of coffee, this time leaving out the heavy cream, and head for the shower.

Josh

"There was a long hard time when I kept far from me the remembrance of what I had thrown away when I was quite ignorant of its worth."
—Charles Dickens, *Great Expectations*

DOES SHE REALLY think she will get away with this? Josh paces the marble floor of the Tuscan-inspired kitchen he and Dillon had planned together in the early years of their marriage. Anger boils inside him. What the hell was she thinking? Canceling his trip to Paris and going there on her own, as if Klein Matthews is going to leave Top Dog Publishing for her no-name startup.

Fury grips him by the throat, and it is all he can do not to slam his fist into the oversized mirror hanging on the main wall of the kitchen. He hates being one-upped by anyone, least of all the wife who chose to leave him.

The nerve required to do what Dillon has done is what gets him the most. What happened to the mousy, no-confidence songwriter who timidly appeared in his office on a winter afternoon, hopeful that he might at least give her some indication she wasn't wasting her time in this town?

Her talent had been undeniable then. It still is, but if Josh regrets anything, it is the fact that he has let her get too sure of herself. Think that she has something, anything really, to do with his success, because nothing could be further from the truth.

He has an enviable roster of songwriters and artists, many of whom perform their own work, unlike Dillon. She's never had the courage to sing her songs, and even though he personally believes she could have made a career as an artist as well, he's never let her get too far with that thinking. He likes keeping the reins a little tight. Likes being the one with the ultimate control in the relationship.

For a long time, Dillon was fine with that. She appreciated a shoulder to lean on, a hand to hold. And, truth be told, if it hadn't been for the changes in her over the last couple of years, that budding confidence that gave her new awareness of her own value to the publishing company, he probably never would have noticed Leanne Henry.

The Vanderbilt intern had certainly noticed him and made no secret of it on the afternoons she appeared at the office to put in the three hours required for her undergraduate degree. The flirtation had started simply enough. Leanne commenting on his cologne, pointing out how nice the color of his shirt was as a contrast to his eyes. And what man didn't like those things? Especially after several years of marriage when neither partner felt the absolute need to go overboard with the compliments and admiration they had once doled out to each other with such generosity.

He hadn't encouraged her at first, enjoyed the attention for sure, but he knew better than to mess with fire, and Leanne Henry was definitely fire.

In fact, as time went on, he reminded himself of one of those poor moths that kamikazed themselves into the flames of the firepit he and Dillon liked to turn on late in the evening with a glass of wine. He'd tried to rescue them numerous times. Not only because he knew it made Dillon see him in a favorable light, but also because he hated to think that any living creature could be so destined for self-destruction. Josh wondered now if he had identified with those poor, doomed moths even then. No, Josh refuses to accept that. True enough, he had flown right into the fire that was Leanne Henry, but he'd be damned if he was going to sacrifice himself to Dillon's wrath as well.

He's worked too long and too hard, accomplished too much to hand any of it over to her. Any more of it than the law requires him to, anyway. He'd hired the best divorce attorney in Nashville, one known to play as dirty as necessary, and he's okay with that.

He has no desire to be cruel. But he's tried to play nice, offering Dillon a few of the artists on the Top Dog roster who, truthfully, would probably end up being dud signs. He isn't about to hand over any of the known names he's put his blood, sweat, and tears into developing.

He opens the set of French doors that lead from the kitchen to the deck overlooking the large expanse of grass, so perfectly manicured it rivals the local golf club's turf. He remembers coming home from the office late one afternoon to find Dillon lying on her back, staring up at the clouds, the green grass a blanket beneath her. That had been in the early days of their marriage when she had been extraordinarily happy to see him at the end of the day.

He'd crept down the stairs, tiptoed across the grass and dropped down to surprise her with a quick kiss. She had laughed, putting her arms around his neck and pulling him to her. Things had gotten hot and heavy there in their backyard. And if she hadn't stood, taking his hand and pulling him across the yard and up the stairs into the house to their bedroom, he could have made love to her right there on the back lawn with any neighbors who wished to see welcome to do so.

That had been the attraction he felt for her back then. He grieved for that feeling sometimes, in moments when his guard was lowered, and he wasn't letting himself think about all the ugly moments that had taken place between them since that afternoon.

Most of them were his fault. He admits that. He'd thought he could have his fling and keep what he had with Dillon at the same time. But could a person really wear two masks requiring such distinctly different emotions?

His sex life with Dillon had been more than enough for him. He couldn't even explain then why the thing with Leanne had gone from zero to sixty practically overnight. The sex with Leanne was a completely different level of expectation from what Dillon had wanted from him. Three and four times a day was more in line with Leanne's needs.

It hadn't taken long for him to begin to feel as if he had signed up for a beginner 5K and found himself in the middle of a throng of New York City marathon runners. Only he wasn't prepared to go twenty-six miles in one stretch. His shoes didn't have that kind of tread. The marathon had been exciting at first, but when it became clear after the first week or so that he would be expected to run that kind of race daily, even the thought of sex began to exhaust him.

He supposed that was what had initially planted a question mark in Dillon's mind. She had noticed his lagging interest and gone out and bought a series of outfits that would have once had him carrying her up the stairs to their bedroom and locking the door.

He'd even gone to his doctor and explained his inability to keep up with his sex life, leaving out the more pertinent details, of course. He let the doctor think he was talking about his performance within his marriage and not the fact that he was having an affair with someone twenty-some years his junior, a young woman he absolutely could not keep up with.

He'd taken his prescription for the little blue pill home, trying it the next day when he thought it might be of the most use. But the thing about Leanne was he never knew when she would pop into his office for a quickie or how many times in one day that might occur. And so there were days when he would find himself trapped at his desk hiding evidence of his readiness even at times when there was no need to be ready.

He drops his head back now, stares up at the clear blue sky above him, and laughs a little. He certainly should be able to laugh at himself. There had been times when it was that ridiculous, and he felt bad for the pain he had caused Dillon.

But does he owe her the business he'd spent his entire adult life growing all because of one bout of incredible stupidity that most people would call a midlife crisis? He doesn't think so.

Maybe he'll call his cutthroat attorney and ask him to lower the heat a bit. All things considered, that is probably fair, but letting Dillon steal Klein Matthews from him, no, that isn't going to happen.

Dillon

"Freedom lies in being bold."

—Robert Frost

TWENTY MINUTES LATER, I feel completely refreshed and wide awake.

The first thing I need to do, the thing I have admittedly been dreading, is to call Klein. No point in putting it off because he'll be expecting Josh to be here. And once he realizes I've come in his place, there will be the obvious questions as to why. Delaying isn't going to lessen the awkwardness of it.

I pick up my phone, tap into Contacts, and scroll for Klein's name, making the call. It's four rings before he answers. I am just about ready to hang up, let cowardice overrule my common-sense resolution to get the initial contact over with.

"Hello?"

I hear the question in the greeting, and I stammer a bit. "H-hello. Klein. It's Dillon. Dillon Blake."

"Hey, Dillon," Klein says cautiously, and I realize how silly I must sound, acting as if he doesn't know who I am.

"So, this is admittedly a little awkward. But here goes. I'm in Paris."

Silence. Pause. "With Josh?"

"No. Actually, it's just me. I came instead of Josh."

"Oh," he says. "Is he coming later or—"

"I don't know."

"Has something happened?" he asks then, a cautious note in his voice.

"Yes. Sort of. Well, yes, it has." I'm rushing my words now. "Josh and I are no longer together. And I'm no longer with Top Dog Publishing."

"Ah." Surprise underlines the response.

I forge on. "So, I was wondering if we could meet today and have a short talk. I promise not to take up much of your time. I know you have the show tonight, and you'll have rehearsals."

"Well, sure," he says. "What did you have in mind?"

"You're staying at the Ritz Paris as well, I believe?"

"Yes."

"I was getting ready to head out and do a little sightseeing. Maybe find a café where we could sit for a bit. Would that be all right?"

"Yeah," he says. "What time would you like to meet?"

"The lobby in half an hour?"

"Ah, sure. Okay. I'll see you there."

"Thank you, Klein."

I put down my phone, exhaling a sigh as if I've been holding my breath for the last few minutes. I guess I'd expected Klein to turn me down. I'm grateful that he didn't, and now I need to make the most of his agreeing to see me.

I glance in the mirror across from the bed at my outfit, trying to decide if the black pants and light blue fitted sweater are a good choice, or if I should find something else from the depths of my suitcase.

I decide on a crisp white cotton shirt, opting to leave my hair loose instead of in a ponytail. I go light on the makeup, but opt to add eyeliner and some mascara, trying not to look too closely at my motivation. Not that it would take a genius to nail it. What woman wouldn't want to look her best in a face to face with Klein? There probably aren't any in actual existence, and I am certainly no exception.

Even so, I also know that vanity aside, my desire to make a good impression on Klein is about business and nothing more. My decision to start my own publishing company with me as my sole client is admittedly a gutsy one. I have a decent cushion for start-up, but that will last only so long, and I feel sure at some point soon I will start to feel the stress of the need to become profitable.

For a moment, I feel a stab of panic for the fact that I have put myself in competition with my cheating ex-husband. Failure is not an option if I intend to have a shred of dignity left.

Was I crazy to set this mountain in front of myself?

Most likely.

Too late now for second thoughts. I take a step back, study myself in the mirror, decide that I look appropriately professional. I reach for my phone and room key, toss them in a small backpack I had planned to use for walking around the city, and leave the room.

Dillon

"I always find it more difficult to say the things I mean than the things I don't."

—W. Somerset Maugham

HE'S WAITING NEAR the front desk when I arrive.

His back is to me, but I have no difficulty recognizing his broad shoulders. "Klein."

He turns at the sound of his name, and for just a millisecond, I have the feeling he is glad to see me. The way you're happy to see someone when you're away from home and spot a person you know.

I remember the first time I saw him, how stunning I'd found him then.

Turns out, that hasn't changed. He has the kind of magnetic good looks that immediately draw the eye. He's six-three or a little better, muscled but lean in the way of a man who knows his way around a gym. Country music fans are as crazy about him as they are Luke Bryan and Holden Ashford.

His trademark wide smile is guarded when he says, "Hey, Dillon. Good to see you."

"You, too," I say, overcome with a sudden urge to giggle like a starstruck fan. I compose myself and add, "Thank you for meeting me."

"Sure. Where would you like to go?"

"Okay if we walk? There's a café not far from here."

He waves a hand for me to lead the way. I struggle to find something to say that doesn't reveal how nervous I am or the fact that my hands are shaking.

We walk side by side through the main door of the hotel and down the street. The sun is bright against a blue sky. The air is warm but without humidity.

"How have you been, Dillon?"

I start to give him a lighthearted response, but something in the weight of the question tempers my answer. "I'm making my way back."

"I'm sorry to hear about you and Josh. I thought y'all were—"

"Me, too. And thanks. It wasn't exactly what I expected. But people change, and sometimes end up being different from what you thought."

"Yeah," he says. "They do."

I want to ask him what he means, but we've reached the entrance to the café, and I walk up to the hostess, asking her if we can have a table outside. And then I remember that Klein might not want to sit in an open area, so I ask him if this is okay.

"It's not a problem," he says.

I notice then that he isn't wearing his customary ball cap. In most of the photos I've seen him in since he got famous, he's worn one pulled low over his eyes, sometimes with sunglasses, sometimes not. I suppose he's not as likely to be recognized here as in the United States.

We sit, and the waitress brings us two menus. I look at Klein. "Early lunch?"

"Sounds good," he says.

"I don't think my body knows what meal it wants, but I'm hungry."

We peruse the menus for a minute, the silence awkward, compelling me to lighten it.

"Are you looking forward to the concert tonight?"

He meets my gaze with a polite answer. "Yes. I'm grateful to have the opportunity. It's an amazing place to be able to play."

"I can't wait to see the show."

"Thanks. For coming, I mean.'"

"Of course," I say, and trail off, awkwardly. I wonder why things feel so strained between us. I try to remember if it ever felt like this when we talked in the past. I don't think so. Admittedly, our conversations have mostly always taken place under the constrains of professional

47

settings and other people being present. But I don't remember ever being this tongue-tied with him.

The waitress returns, and I order a green salad and the braised artichokes. Klein asks for the mozzarella cream tagliatelle.

We make small talk for a few minutes, and I remember the way he has of turning the conversation back to the person he is talking to, making it about them as much as he can. I wonder where he learned this, or if he knows how much it makes others like him.

"Are you writing much these days?" he asks.

"Not as much as I'd like to be. The brain isn't cooperating. I guess it's the separation and life being in flux."

"Temporary writer's block, I'm sure."

"Have you ever had it?"

He hesitates, glances off, and then says, "Yeah. Kind of been going through that for a while now myself."

"I'm sorry," I say, surprised, wondering what the reason is. I find myself wanting to reassure him. "I've talked to a few writer friends about it, and everyone seems to have a slightly different take on what to do."

He appears to consider this, and then, "I'm not sure there is anything to do about it. I don't feel like I have anything to write about anymore."

I'm a little taken aback by the admission. "You're too young for that," I say, surprised by the adamance in his voice. I understand my own currently dry well. Disillusion. Disappointment. Betrayal. I have every intention of getting over it, if for no other reason than to show Josh I don't need him. But I hear something different in Klein's voice. And I'm not sure what to make of it.

The waitress arrives with our food, disrupting our conversation. We watch as she places the beautiful plates before us, the food arranged in colorful proportions designed to make the mouth water at the sight of it. She pours us each another glass of mineral water, asks if there's anything else she can get us in beautifully accented English. We both say no at the same time, and with a smile, she leaves the table.

"This looks wonderful," I say.

"Yeah, the food here is really something."

"Have you been to Paris before?"

"No. First time."

"Anywhere else in the country?"

"First trip to Europe, actually."

"If you have the time, you should see some of the countryside," I say. "You can pretty much get off the train in any small town and end up thinking it's the best place you've ever been."

He hesitates, and then, "I'd love to do that, but I'll be heading back to Nashville once the show is over."

"Ah," I say. I pick up my fork, and at my cue, Klein does the same. "So, what's next for you when you leave here?"

He toys with the pasta, twisting it around the end of his fork. "I'm still trying to figure that out."

"More touring scheduled?"

"Not right at the moment."

"Maybe that will give you some time to get back to writing. I know how hard it is to be creative when you're on the road."

"Yeah," he says. "I'm not feeling that too much these days, either."

I put down my fork, listening for the undercurrent beneath his admission. Something is different with him. There's a sadness in his voice I've never heard before. "Is everything okay, Klein?"

"I think I just need a break," he says. "Some space to, I don't know, get my feet back on the ground, I guess."

"Are you planning to take some time off?"

"I am."

"A few weeks of vacation can be just the thing sometimes. We all need a reset now and then."

He's silent for several moments, and I feel there's more that he wants to say but is reluctant to do so. When he finally replies, his voice is low and sure. "I think this is going to be my last show."

I stare at him, shocked, not sure what to make of the statement.

Before I can respond, he adds, "I don't know if I want to do this anymore."

"Perform you mean?"

"That, yeah, and as far as the writing, I'm pretty sure I don't have anything to say that's relevant to what life means anyway."

I debate my response because I have no idea where this is coming from, what's happened in his life to bring him to this place. "I think your songs are relevant to a lot of people, Klein."

"They're entertainment," he says with a shrug. "Nothing more. There's nothing wrong with entertainment. I understand that people need it. I need it. An escape here and there. But in the big picture, it won't mean anything. No permanent marks left for others to follow."

I lift my glass, take a sip of the cold mineral water, try to sort my response into something that won't be about me. "What's happened, Klein?"

He shrugs. "I'm just seeing life a little differently these days," he says. "I chased after this thing for a long time, and I don't know what I thought it would do for me. Make me happy, I guess. And there are moments of that, for sure. It's been a pretty incredible ride. But when it gets right down to it, it hasn't made me into a better person. I'm pretty sure it's made me a worse person."

"I don't know what you're using for a gauge of comparison, but I'm aware of some of the things you've done for other people, Klein, and you've used a lot of what you've achieved for good."

51

"With money, that's not that hard."

"Not everyone sees it that way," I say. "There are a lot of people who aren't as willing to share their good fortune with others."

He shrugs. "At some point along the way, I let it all go to my head. I started to believe that good wasn't good enough. That maybe I needed perfect."

I place my fork on my plate, brush my hand across my napkin. "Is this about the breakup with Riley?"

"I don't know if it's as much about the breakup as it is about why I broke up with her. And something that happened because of it."

I want to ask him what, but I force myself not to because I have a feeling it is deeply personal. And now doesn't seem like the time. "It would be a great loss for you to give up your music. What if you just took some time off and looked at it fresh in a couple of months?"

He shrugs, shakes his head a little. "It doesn't feel like that will make a difference." He looks at me for a moment and then, "What is it you wanted to see me about, Dillon?"

I consider not telling him now because, in light of what he's just shared with me, it's almost certainly pointless. It seems shallow, as well. I draw in a deep breath, a flutter of awkwardness in my stomach. I decide to jump in, drop the pretense of beating around the bush. "I'm thinking about starting my own company. I've asked Josh for the rights to all of my songs. I'm no longer under contract with him."

I can see I've surprised him. "That's probably a good thing," Klein says, measured.

"Yeah." I hesitate, looking for the right words. "I wanted to see you because I'm hoping you might consider moving to my new publishing house."

"Oh." His surprise is clear. "I'm happy for you, Dillon. I think you'll do well. I feel sure a good number of Josh's writers are there because of you. I was certainly one of them."

I know this to be true, but even so, hearing him say it surprises me a little. "It was just lucky for me that I was at the Bluebird that night. Someone else would have signed you for sure."

"Maybe. But I don't know that I would have taken their offer the way I did with you."

The admission forms a connection between us that is nearly tangible. I want to latch on to it, use it as leverage for the hope that Klein will somehow renew his love for the music that got him to where he is today. "I know this thing we do cannot be just about success. Once you've achieved a certain level of that, the focus shifts back to a need for it to mean something. For it to matter somehow in the big picture."

"Has that been true for you?" he asks.

"Yeah. It has. Being named songwriter of the year was something bigger than anything I had allowed myself to dream. But after that, I went through this period where I felt like whatever I was writing had to do more than make the top of a chart. I wanted to know that I had something to say that would move someone. Make them feel like they weren't as alone as they thought they were. And for a while, I couldn't write anything that lived up to that."

"What changed that? Why are you still writing?"

I consider this for a moment, but the answer is easy. "Because I don't know who I am without it."

I see that this resonates with him, recognize the flare of kinship in his eyes. "I've been trying to picture who I'll be after all this. I have to admit it's not clear."

"Is there anything else you've ever wanted to do?"

"Not that I can remember," he says, his expression resigned to the fact that he'll most likely be lost without this thing that has been his identity as writing has been mine.

I want to find the words to convince him that leaving his music behind would be a mistake, but I can't dig anything up from the well of disappointment inside me. Even as I wonder if it is entirely selfish, I realize I feel the kind of grief I am sure most of his fans will feel at the thought of him no longer making the music they have loved from him. But something tells me that arguing this point right now isn't the thing to do. And so I drop it under the realization that maybe what Klein needs is a friend. Someone to listen, hear what it is that has brought him to this point.

"What time do you have to be at rehearsal?" I ask.

"Four o'clock," he says.

"Well, you have a few hours until then. Would you like to look around the city with me?"

He hesitates. I force myself to let him make the call without any further prodding from me.

"I thought I might visit the Louvre this afternoon." He glances down, suddenly awkward. "I know. I don't look like the museum type."

I smile a little. "Another layer. I like it."

"Join me?"

My pulse skitters at the thought of actually getting to spend more time with him. "I'd love to. It's been on my list, and I never made it there when I was here before."

"Okay, then," he says. "Would you like anything else?"

"No. I'm good. That was wonderful."

He signals the waitress for the check and insists on paying the bill against my protests. When she returns with his receipt, she smiles a shy smile and says, "Would you mind giving me your autograph?"

Klein is gracious. "Ah, no, I don't mind at all."

She hands him a card with the restaurant's logo on the front.

He turns it over on the back and asks what her name is.

"Aimeé," she says, again shy.

"That's pretty," he says, writing her name on the card

and then scrawling his signature beneath. "Thank you, Aimeé."

"Non. Merci beaucoup." She presses the card into her palm and wishes us both a good day.

"Nice to be recognized in Paris," I say, noting his discomfort with the attention.

"Yeah, I was a little surprised to see we have fans here."

"Power of streaming. And judging by the fact that the concert is sold out, I would say you do."

His smile is marked by humility, when he says, "We better head for the museum."

I reach for my purse, and we both stand. I do notice as we're leaving the restaurant that Aimeé lets her gaze follow him to the front and out the door. I completely understand.

Dillon

"If you don't know history, then you don't know anything. You are a leaf that doesn't know it is part of a tree. "

—Michael Crichton

THE TAXI DROPS us at the Louvre. We stand for a moment, taking in the majestic building before us.

"It's huge," Klein says.

"It is," I say, nodding in agreement. "So while we were driving, I googled for a refresher on the history of the Louvre. It was built as a fortress around 1190 and then rebuilt in the sixteenth century to become a royal palace. Apparently, every ruler kept making it bigger until Louis the fourteenth made Versailles the royal palace."

"Guess this one wasn't impressive enough," Klein says, shaking his head.

"Out with the old. In with the new."

He smiles at this, and we walk to the ticket entrance.

We end up waiting in line for nearly thirty minutes. We learn that we won't be able to see the Mona Lisa, because the only way to do so is by online reservation. Meanwhile, we ogle the architecture of the building, marveling that such elaborate engineering could have been done so many hundreds of years ago.

"They had a lot figured out back then, didn't they?" Klein says as we finally step inside the entrance.

"More than we give them credit for," I agree, noticing a couple of girls staring at Klein. One taps her phone screen, and types in something, leans in and shows it to the other girl. They whisper back and forth before finally getting up the courage to walk over. The braver one of the two steps forward, flipping her long dark hair over her shoulder as she says in American-accented English, "Hi, Klein! We both love your music and have tickets to your concert tonight."

The friend standing behind her giggles, obviously nervous. "We were wondering if we might get your autograph."

Klein smiles a smile I'm sure he's given to too many fans to count. It's a smile that immediately puts the young girl at ease, tells her she's not foolish for approaching him. "Sure," he says. "What would you like me to write it on?"

"Ah, oh, gosh," the girl says. "Maybe the back of my T-shirt?"

"That's fine," he says, smiling in a way that puts her at ease.

She shrugs out of her leather jacket, turning her back to him. Her friend passes a Sharpie, which she's dug from the bottom of a backpack. Klein glances at me with an apology in his eyes. I shrug, shake my head. It's part of what he does, and I'm actually happy to see him getting recognition for his talent, although I'm sure the girls' interest in him includes the fact that he's so easy on the eyes.

Klein writes something and then scrawls his signature across the middle of her back. She turns to thank him when he's done. "Would you mind doing one for my friend? She's too shy to ask."

"Of course," he says.

The other girl steps around her friend and displays the back of her T-shirt, giggling as she does.

"We can't wait to hear you tonight," she says.

"Well, I certainly appreciate both of you planning to be at the concert. Where are you from?"

"North Carolina," she says. "We're here on tour with our college debate team. We heard you were going to be playing while we were in Paris, so we begged our professor for permission to get tickets. Luckily, he's cool and agreed."

Klein hands her the marker back and says, "Lucky for me."

Both girls giggle now, the more daring one giving me a look of envy. I start to reassure her that she has nothing to worry about, but press my lips together and keep silent.

"Okay, then, we'll see you tonight, Klein. We'll be waving from the audience."

"I'll be watching for you. Thanks again."

"No. Thank you," the two girls say in unison, turning around to skip off.

"Does that ever get old?" I ask him once the girls are out of earshot.

"Ah, it's not something I think I'll ever get used to," he admits.

"How so?"

"Well, being recognized for one thing. And I always want to look over my shoulder to make sure they're not talking to someone else."

I smile. "Yeah, I get that, but by now, you should know you have a lot of admirers."

He shrugs, drops his chin. I realize he really isn't comfortable with fame. "You don't need to feel guilty about it, you know."

He lifts his gaze, stares off into the crowd for a moment, and says, "Sometimes, I do. I don't know. People do far more important things in this world than sing. And yet, I get so much recognition for it, not to mention the money."

"People like to be entertained," I say. "There's nothing

wrong with that. You let people escape for a little while into something they enjoy. Put aside the realities of life."

He looks down and then meets my gaze. "I get all that. That's what music has always done for me, but somehow being on this end of it, there are times when I wonder how justified it is."

The line has started to move, and within a couple of minutes, we are standing in an enormous open area that appears to be the center of things. Since we're short on time, we agree to do the Richelieu wing and tour the French paintings on level two.

We follow the brochure map and then take a staircase up. We start in Room 1, standing and staring at the artwork hanging wall to wall. I sense that Klein is as awestruck as I am. We amble room to room for the next twenty minutes, saying little, each of us lost in our own wonder at the masterful works surrounding us.

I stop in front of one painting. The title reads, *Trussing Hay*. I stare at the people captured lifelike in their work.

I look at Klein, and ask, "Do you think the artists here were aware of their talent or saw it as something that would be revered hundreds of years after they completed it?"

"Some of them, maybe, but I kind of think most of them would be amazed to know that anything they created could have such a long life. And too, I doubt many of them actually earned a lot of money for their art."

"No," I agree. "Probably not. It's kind of hard to understand why it would be nearly priceless now and virtually worthless at the time it was created."

"That's one of the reasons why I don't think of what I do as art," he says. "I would never compare myself with any of the artists here."

"'But then we've just acknowledged that most of them probably never saw themselves like that at all."

We walk on into another room and spend the next hour and a half absorbing all that we can. It's almost three o'clock when Klein glances at his watch and says, "I hate to go, but I have rehearsal in thirty minutes."

"Oh, of course," I say. "I'll walk out with you."

We follow the signs to the exit and find ourselves in the pyramid courtyard. "I'll get an Uber to rehearsals."

"Okay," I say. "I'll head back to the hotel then."

He hesitates for a moment, and then says, "Would you like to come with me? If you're not doing anything else, I mean."

I could deny the flood of happiness surging through me, but who would I be kidding? Klein Matthews just asked me to go to his rehearsal. I'm as giddy inside as the teenagers asking for his autograph. But I manage to sound like it's no big deal. "Ah, no, actually, that would be great," I say. "I would love to come."

Dillon

"Music is a writer's heartbeat."

—A.D. Posey

THE MERCEDES UBER weaves us in and out of Paris traffic, getting us to the rehearsal hall in fifteen minutes. The driver drops us at a side entrance per Klein's request. Klein texts someone, telling me, "They'll be down in just a minute to let us in."

A few seconds later, the door opens, and Klein's manager, Curtis Bartholomew, greets us with a smile. "Hey, man. Oh, wait, Dillon. Where did you come from?"

"Staying at the same hotel," I say. "Klein was kind enough to invite me to watch y'all do your thing."

"It's good to see you," Curtis says, squeezing my shoulder. He's tall, six-four or so, without the cowboy hat he's known for wearing around Nashville.

"No hat," I say, smiling.

"Yeeeaah, it just didn't quite go with the whole Parisian thing."

I laugh. "If anyone can pull it off, Curtis, you can."

He smiles. "Everybody's already set up and waiting, Klein. We'll try to keep this to a minimum. Save your pipes for tonight."

"Thanks," Klein says. "I think there are just a couple of songs that could use a redo. The new stuff."

"It sounded great to me last time I heard it," Curtis says.

We take a flight of stairs to the third floor. Curtis leads the way, opening a set of double doors into a room with a very high ceiling. Klein's bandmates fill the room, most of whom I recognize from various encounters in Nashville. Everyone waves, friendly, smiling.

"Hey, guys," Klein says. "We were doing a little tour of the Louvre."

Hank Morgan, the band's lead guitar player, grins and says, "Oh, now, Klein's gonna go getting all cultured."

"The only culture you know about, Hank," Peggy Simmons, one of the backup singers, says, "is the kind you find in buttermilk."

The room erupts in laughter. Klein slaps Hank on the shoulder, and says, "I'm afraid your reputation precedes you, buddy."

"What the heck's wrong with buttermilk?" Hank tosses back. "Y'all land in France and start thinking you're all hoity-toity."

More laughter, and I stand back, taking in how comfortable everyone seems to be with one another.

I've witnessed it a few times before. When the band members have been harmoniously chosen, the feeling is like that of a family. Everyone knows their roles, where they fit in, and how to interact with one another. Klein, of course, is head of the family. And I can see that he is well-loved by the members of his band. With the polite manners that are one of his trademarks, Klein leads me over to a leather sofa and asks if I would like anything to drink.

"I'm fine. Thank you. Please, do whatever you need to do. Ignore me. I'll just be taking it all in."

Klein picks up his guitar, strums a few chords, and then steps up to the microphone. "All right. Two or three run-throughs of those songs I keep messing up, and that ought to do it before the show. Everybody in agreement?"

"Yeah, man," a couple of voices ring out.

"Let's do it," Klein says.

All said and done, they play for forty-five minutes or so. It feels a bit like I'm watching a reality series. Klein has a couple of real comedians in his band. There's as much laughter going on as there is singing and playing. But I know the final run-through when I hear it. The three songs they end with are as smooth and perfectly rendered as any master recording I've ever heard.

I watch Klein deliver the words to each of the songs

he's written, and I'm as mesmerized, hanging on each and every syllable, as I know his fans will be tonight.

Once they've strummed the last note, Curtis walks over, sits down next to me, arms folded across his chest, and says, "So what did you think?"

"Incredible," I say.

"They are, aren't they?"

"Yeah. The fans will get what they came for."

A stretch of awkward silence settles between us, and I sense he wants to ask me something.

"So," he says, "you mind if I ask what's going on with you and Josh?"

The bluntness of the question would be offensive except for the fact I know Curtis is asking out of Klein's best interests, representing his client first and foremost.

"We're getting a divorce," I say.

"I'm sorry to hear that, Dillon. Except for the fact that I always thought you were too nice for him."

I lean back a little, not hiding my surprise.

"Well," he says, "everybody knows Josh is out for Josh. Surely, you knew that, too."

"I found that out, but no, I can't say that I knew that in the beginning."

"Hey, I'm sorry. I didn't mean to sound so harsh. Divorce is a bitch. Believe me, I know."

I soften. I'd heard about Curtis's experience. His wife had decided she didn't want to be married anymore but also wanted to leave the marriage with more than her share. She'd hired a shark of an attorney, and the rumor mill had suggested her efforts paid off.

"It can get ugly, I hate to tell you," he says. "You got yourself a good attorney? Can't recommend that highly enough," he adds with a twinge of sarcasm underlining the words.

"From all indications, yes," I say, hating the ick factor of the mercenary aspect of ending a marriage.

"Yeah, I never imagined mine would end up the way it did," Curtis says. "I don't think any of us do. But when one half decides they're not happy anymore, and you realize there's nothing you can do to fix it, you need to get off the boat with a life vest."

I smile, nodding a little. "I'm pretty sure Josh would just as soon see me drown."

"You gonna take him for half the business?"

"I'm planning to strike out on my own."

"Taking any clients with you?" Curtis asks, the glint in his eye telling me the real motivation behind his questioning.

"Would I like to take Klein with me? Yes. Of course, I would. Who wouldn't? Do I expect that to actually happen? Probably not."

Curtis looks at me for a few long seconds. "Josh know about these aspirations of yours?"

"He does."

"And I'm surprised we haven't already heard about this."

"He's probably hoping I'm bluffing."

"Or maybe he's afraid Klein would be all for it?"

I meet his knowing gaze, a little surprised. "I'm not assuming that."

"It's no secret Josh can be an ass. I'd be hard-pressed to say we enjoy working with him."

This surprises me, I have to admit. Josh puts on a good front, wining and dining, kissing butts at whatever level it needs to be done to ascertain the complete happiness of his clients. "You still planning on writing once you start up your own publishing company?"

"I'm not sure I know how not to write," I say, smiling a little. "Some days, I'd like to go that route. Quit trying to outbest myself."

"You've set a high bar, that's for sure," he says. "You've written some great songs."

"Thank you."

"Really. You have. Whatever else you decide to pursue in life, surely you know that?"

"I appreciate that, Curtis. It's a competitive business, as you know."

"That it is. The bar gets higher every day. But I enjoy chasing that. Trying to figure out what will resonate as the cool new sound. Keeping enough of the old school in it to keep the traditional fans happy."

"Y'all are certainly doing a great job of that."

"Well," he says, standing and slapping his hands on his knees. "I've got some loose ends to tie up before tonight. Anytime you want to talk, you've got my number. Whether it's about business or if I can help you navigate the divorce waters, I'll be happy to tell you anything I've learned."

"Thanks, Curtis," I say, sincerely appreciating the offer. "That means a lot. It feels a little overwhelming at the moment."

"I know. Figuring out how to separate a life you lived as one with someone into two separate lives again is no easy trick."

Klein walks over and says, "I think I'm going to head back to the hotel, grab a shower. Maybe close my eyes for thirty minutes or so. Still feeling that jet lag."

I stand and say, "Okay. I'm ready to head back. Mind if we share a ride?"

"Absolutely."

We tell everyone goodbye and head downstairs.

"So, what'd you think?" Klein asks as we reach the exit onto the street. "Honestly."

"Honestly? I think you're going to knock it out of the ballpark tonight. You are hitting on all cylinders, Klein. Really."

"That's kind."

"I'm not just being kind. You're writing crazy good

songs. And I could sit and listen to you sing them all day long."

He smiles at this, and I realize maybe I've given away a little too much, but I'm not backtracking any of it because it's true. I could. "I'm no different from anyone else who's bought a ticket to see you tonight."

He's already ordered the Uber, and a black sedan pulls up alongside the curb. Klein opens the back door, waits for me to get in. Once the driver has eased back into traffic, he looks at me and says, "You have no idea how much that means, coming from you."

I lean back, study him for a moment. "You don't see yourself that way, do you?"

He lifts his shoulders in a shrug. "I mean, I understand what it takes to make it in this business, and that I have most of that on a good day. But, no, I have plenty of doubt, that's for sure. Especially before a big show like this."

"That's understandable, but you take to that stage tonight what you had in there this afternoon, and you won't have a single regretting fan."

The driver circles the car to the front of the hotel. Klein thanks him. We slide out of the back, walking through the main entrance and down the long corridor to the elevator that leads to our rooms. We reach my floor first.

"Thanks," Klein says. "It was a great day. I really enjoyed it."

"Me, too," I say. "Thank you for letting me watch the rehearsal."

"My pleasure. I'm heading over at six-thirty. The show starts at eight. Do you want to ride with me, or—"

I want to. I very much want to. But somehow I feel like maybe it will be better for him to be alone in the ride over, have the time to mentally prep for the show. "I'd love to," I say. "But I have a few things I need to do. Emails and stuff."

"Oh. Okay. No problem. So wish me luck?"

"Good luck," I say. "Not that you need it. Okay, then. See you." And I head for my room before I can change my mind.

Klein

"There is a charm about the forbidden that makes it
unspeakably desirable."

—Mark Twain

IT AMAZES ME that I still get this nervous before a show.

I don't know why, really, because I can mostly do it with my eyes closed I've done it so many times. I think what gets me is the expectation of giving people what they've come for, and I have to admit I'm never one hundred percent certain I'll be able to do that. It's as if every time is the first time.

Inside my room, I consider taking a nap first but then decide on the shower since I feel completely wide awake now. I stand beneath the pulsating spray, letting it beat against my face, trying to blank my mind of everything except what's before me tonight.

But my thoughts go immediately to Riley, and then I

realize that for most of the time I have been with Dillon today, the awful sense of anguish I've been feeling got put on hold for a little while at least. Thinly veiled, but still not at the front of my thoughts as it has been for weeks now.

The finality of Riley's decision is the weight I can't seem to get off my chest. I recognize the emotion as grief. As full-blown and devastating as if I had actually known and held in my arms the child the two of us made together. Somehow, not having known that small life seems worse.

I get out of the shower, towel off, and walk back into the bedroom. I drop onto the bed and stare at the ceiling, contemplating the one thing I know I should not be considering doing before a concert. But of its own volition, my hand reaches for my phone on the nightstand. I click into the Home screen, tap phone, and then Riley's name in the list of recent calls. My heart pounds as I listen to it ring. I want her to pick up and yet dread the fact that she might do so.

"Hello."

When her voice comes across the line, I close my eyes, drawing in a deep breath. "Hey."

"Hey," she says. It's clear that she's not happy to hear from me.

"Do you have a minute to talk?" I ask.

"What is there to talk about, Klein? I think everything has been said, hasn't it?"

"No, actually, it hasn't."

"You've said everything you needed to say, right?"

"Riley, I don't want to fight with you. That's not why I called."

"Then why?"

"Because. . .I don't know. I can't stop thinking about—"

"Just stop, Klein. There's nothing to think about. It's done. Over. There's nothing you can do to change it."

I press my lips together, suppressing the instant knife of rage that slices through my chest. What I really want to do is ask her how she could have done such a thing. But I know that won't change anything, so I say in as even a voice as I can manage, "Are you okay?"

"I'm fine, Klein. It's not as if you care about me. If this is about your guilt, you need to just let it go. If it makes you feel any better, I didn't give you a choice in the matter."

"It doesn't make me feel better at all," I say.

"You're at the top of the world, Klein. You don't need me. You made that very clear. Enjoy your life. Enjoy what you made for yourself. And don't call me again. Please."

The resounding click in my ear tells me she's hung up. "Damn." I shout the word, hurling my phone across the room where it bounces off the far wall and lands on the rug-covered floor with a thud.

My chest tightens, and it feels as if my heart will beat a hole in my chest. What had I expected, though? I'm the one who broke up with her. I'm the one who told her we didn't have a future.

If I hadn't ended things with her, would she have made a different choice? Yes, I know she would have. So how can I be angry with her? She's right not to want to see me again. I put her in the position of having to make an awful choice. *I* did that.

A bottle of wine and two glasses sit on a table a few yards away from the bed. Funny, I hadn't paid any attention to the bottle until now. But that's what usually does it, me getting on fire about something and wanting to squelch the flames with the one thing I know for sure will put them out.

I consider getting up and opening it. Chasing away the terrible fury eating me alive, if only temporarily. But then I think about the show tonight and how I cannot arrive there drunk. It's not as if it hasn't happened before, but I owe my band more than that. I owe them the promise I made the last time it happened.

A memory of the rehab center where I'd done my last dry-out rises up and slams me with a wave of nausea.

The only comparison I have for detox is the images of hell I grew up envisioning in my small South Carolina Baptist church. Listening to my own body scream for even an ounce of alcohol to dull the pain was as close to being consumed with Satan's flames as I can imagine.

I glance at the bottle again. The pull is strong. So strong that I do not trust myself to ignore it.

I don't trust myself to stay here alone.

Granted, me getting drunk would provide ample evidence to everyone in the band that I've gone off the wagon, but even so, I know the best thing I can do for myself is to not be alone.

I get dressed for the gig, throwing my clothes on as fast as I can. And then I grab my slightly dented phone and head for the door.

Dillon

"I dwell in possibility."

—Emily Dickinson

THE KNOCK ON the door surprises me. Maybe it's housekeeping to do the turndown service, but it seems a little early for that. I peer through the peephole to see Klein standing in the hallway. I turn the deadbolt and open the door. "Hey," I say. "What's up?"

"I know you said you had some work to do, but would you mind if I just hung out in your room for a little bit until it's time to leave for the show?"

"Sure," I say, surprised, but waving a hand for him to come in. "Is everything okay?"

"Yeah, nerves, I guess."

"I was just getting in the shower, but if you'd like to take a nap on the bed or something, I'll be glad to wake you up whenever you want to get ready to leave."

"Thanks," he says. "That actually sounds really good."

I grab the robe from the corner of the bed and head for the bathroom, closing the door quietly behind me. I lean my head back, blow out a breath. That, I had not expected.

Something is wrong. I can feel it, the tension emanating from Klein, but somehow I don't think I should ask. At least not now. It feels like maybe he just needs a safe space, although I can't imagine why or what would make him seek it out here in my room.

I undress, notably conscious of the fact that Klein is on the other side of this door. I stare at my naked self in the oversized mirror above the sink and wonder when I last felt beautiful. It occurs to me with some clarity that at some point in my marriage, I stopped thinking of myself as beautiful at all.

In the beginning, Josh couldn't get enough of me. That had always made me feel good, especially since I had been completely impressed by Josh and his success in the town I so badly wanted to make it in as well. His desire for me had lasted the first couple of years of our marriage.

And then around year three, I had started to feel something a little different, noticed how his gaze always seemed to find the most attractive woman in whatever restaurant we were eating in or party we attended.

At some point along the way, I began to realize it was not my imagination. I tried to renew his interest, did the obligatory Google search for ways to fan the embers of a waning physical attraction. I had been embarrassed for myself as my fingers moved across the keys entering first one phrase, then the next, until I had accumulated a long list of sure-to-succeed recommendations. I am nothing if not determined, though, so I started at the top and worked my way through at least fifteen different foolproof methods for reviving a partner's interest. Each of them worked temporarily. Still, none of them prevented Josh from staring at a woman he obviously found beautiful. But then the final straw had come when I got sick.

I study my reflection, wondering if Klein finds me attractive. Hardly. Good grief, he could have pretty much his pick from women far younger than me. Far hotter than me. Forget that. I turn on the shower, wait a few moments, and then step under the spray, letting the cold water wash the heat from my cheeks.

Once I'm done, I decide to go ahead and get dressed, not wanting to go back into the bedroom on the off chance that Klein has decided to take a nap before the show.

I blow-dry my hair, taking the time to straighten it with a flat iron and then spending way more effort on my makeup than I usually would. Call it vanity, but knowing that I will be among Klein's throng of adoring fans makes me want to try a little harder anyway. I've been in the bathroom for an hour or a little more when I'm finally ready and decide to stick my head out to see if Klein is awake. He is, and standing by the window, hands shoved in the pockets of his jeans.

He turns when I fully open the door and says, "Hey."

"Did you get a little bit of a nap?"

"I did. Should help tonight."

"Is everything all right?" I ask, cautious.

"Yeah," he says. "There are just times when I know I do better not being alone."

Well, I can certainly identify with that. Klein looks as if he wants to elaborate, say more. I instinctively wait.

"I don't know if you heard about my stint in rehab. Or if you knew I had a drinking problem."

The shame in his voice ties a knot in my heart. "There were rumors. I didn't know if any of them were true."

He laughs a short laugh. "I imagine most of them were."

"Are you okay?"

He looks at me then, and I can see in his eyes that he is surprised I've asked. "I am. I mean I think so. To be honest, the reason I came to your room is because I was tempted to pour myself a drink. I know it will temporarily make me quit thinking about things I don't want to think about."

"But that's only temporary, right?"

"Right."

"What can I do?" I ask, wanting to be the shoulder he needs to lean into right now. And then I find myself confiding, "My dad was an alcoholic."

His eyes widen. "Oh. I didn't know that."

"Yeah. It's not something I let myself think about too

often. He died when I was four. In a DUI accident. That he caused."

I feel Klein's shock. He looks as if he has no idea what to say to this. "I'm sorry, Dillon," he says.

"Me, too. I'm sorry he never got help. Or that no one in his life gave him that ultimatum. It was one of my mother's biggest regrets."

"Alcoholics can't be helped until they want to be helped," Klein says quietly.

"There's guilt nonetheless," I say. And then, "You did get help, Klein. That's the part that matters. Not what came before. We're strongest when we turn our back on our weaknesses. That's what you've done. But when you need someone to talk you down from that ledge, you can always call me. Anytime at all."

"Thank you," he says, his gratitude evident in the two words. We hold each other's gaze for a couple of long seconds, and I feel the clicking of a connection between us. Understanding of something that can only happen when two people have experienced a similar pain.

Klein shakes his head a little and says, "I guess I need to head on over. Would you like to go with me now?"

"Yeah," I say, realizing I've been hoping for this all along. "I'm ready, actually."

"You look beautiful, by the way," he says, his gaze again settling fully on my face. I feel heat flood my cheeks, drop my gaze like a high school version of myself, and say, "Thanks."

"No. Really," he says, "you do."

I settle on the option of silence, because I can't think of anything to say that would make me sound less than awkward.

"I'll go ahead and get us a car," Klein says, waving his phone.

"Great," I say, "let me just grab my purse and a jacket."

He waits for me by the door, and as I walk past him, I notice his cologne, how good it smells, and how perfectly it matches my sense of him. I imagine pressing my face to his chest and breathing in that heady scent.

Okay, where had that come from? I give myself a mental swat and head for the elevator, pressing the down button and waiting with my back to him.

"I hope this goes well tonight," he says softly.

I turn then to see the worry in his eyes. "It will. Do you always get nerves before a show?"

"Sometimes more than others," he says, "but playing in a place like this for the first time is a little newly intimidating."

"I can understand that," I say, "but you've got this."

"Thanks, Dillon," he says. He glances off and then back, his eyes direct on mine. "I'm happy we ran into each other here, that it worked out like this."

"Yeah," I say, unable to deny the thrill his words send through me. "Me, too."

Dillon

"Don't we all wish to be seen? Truly seen?"
—Unknown

I AM AT ONE END of the front row. The ticket price for this seat would have been at least six hundred dollars. I'm surrounded by mostly French teenagers, although I hear some native English mixed in with the conversations taking place around me.

"He is so hot." And, "What do you think he would do if I threw my bra at him?" Then, "I don't know, but I might throw my thong."

I nearly laugh at this one, picturing Klein with a pink thong lassoing his guitar.

I try to remember what it was like to be seventeen and within reach of a star as well-known as Klein. I'm pretty sure I never was, but if I had been, I would not have had the confidence to throw my bra or underwear at him.

But I can certainly understand that level of desire to get his attention.

He's wearing faded jeans that fit him like they'd been made specifically for him. They hug his hips, his legs in a way that draws the eye to him and demands that it linger. His shirt is light blue, open collar, and is a near-perfect match to his eyes. Even if Klein hadn't been blessed with a voice that froze a listener into mesmerization, his looks alone would do it.

That's where I am right now. Klein's voice is nirvana. I'm pretty sure I could stand here listening to him forever.

The song is one he wrote. It's one of his number one singles. There's no mystery as to why it hit the top of the charts. All around me, women are standing entranced, no longer chatting and plotting about ways to get his attention. I imagine they're feeling what I'm feeling. Complete captivation. And the undeniable wish that I was the only woman to whom he was singing.

He makes it seem that way, even if it's so obviously not true.

I absorb every word of the song, every note of the melody.

It is utterly beautiful.

Because Top Dog published the song, I know the story behind it. It's about a first love, and just hearing the way Klein sings the words of heartbreak, it's impossible to believe it isn't about Klein's first love. I feel the loss in his voice, see the longing in his eyes. And I wonder what it would be like to be loved by him, with that intensity, that passion.

The last notes of the song fade into silence. There's a full, weighted moment in which the floor area is entirely still.

I stare at Klein, and then his gaze swings to me, deliberate, full of something I don't have the courage to identify.

Surely, I am mistaken. Something in my stomach goes liquid and melts inside me. The woman standing next to me looks at me and says in an awestruck voice, "Lucky you."

I feel myself blush, hot, and flaming. I force indifference into my voice when I say, "I'm sure that's all part of the show. Give a girl what she paid for."

"Ah, no," she says on a knowing laugh. "I'm pretty sure that one was all for you."

When Klein finishes his last song, I leave my seat, needing to get outside into the fresh air. I feel as if I have been infused with heat from the very center of my being. I make my way down the aisle to the exit doors, sweat beading between my breasts and across my forehead. I push them open and then all but run down the corridor past the concession area to the doors that lead outside into the blissfully cool night air.

I walk past a couple of teenagers smoking and find a spot

in the shadows to lean against a wall with my head back, pulling in a few deep breaths.

What. The. Heck.

It had to be precisely what I'd said. Part of the show. He'd just chosen me as the target tonight.

He should be an actor. That was Academy Award caliber stuff. Totally believable. As in, I had believed it. Bought it hook, line, and sinker.

Good grief. Maybe I'm just lonely. Maybe it's the rejection of being tossed aside for a younger model that is finally getting to me. A younger, thinner, more up-to-date model.

Is Klein feeling sorry for me? My cheeks flare in new mortification.

My phone dings. I glare at the screen.

Come backstage. I left word with Mike at the door.

My heart does a ridiculous gallop against the wall of my chest.

I want to.

How could I not want to?

Do I think it's wise at this point?

No. I don't.

I stare at the screen for another moment, then type.

Your show was truly incredible. I'm exhausted. I think I'll catch a cab back to the hotel. Thank you so much for the incredible seat.

I hit send.

Why don't you just write a book, Dillon?

I stare at my phone while he types.

Are you sure?

I hesitate, feel myself leaning into the pull to change my mind. Klein Matthews just asked you to join him backstage. What are you doing, Dillon?

Exercising common sense. Reluctant as I am to do so. I really want to be young and foolish. Except I'm not that young. Old enough to know where foolish will get me.

I'm an old fogey. Beauty rest and all that. Good night.

His reply is several seconds coming.

Okay. Good night.

Regret washes over me in an instant wave. I choke it back and stalk down a taxi. It takes several minutes, and when I finally sink into the back seat and manage to murmur, "Ritz Paris," I don't even care that the driver gives me a suspicious glare, as if he thinks I'm coked up or something.

I ride most of the drive with my eyes closed, trying not to conjure up that moment at the concert when Klein had directed those lyrics at me.

That night we met
I should have made you mine
Not now, not yet
Like I had all the time
In the world, girl

In the world, girl

I sigh and turn my gaze to the window and the city flowing by. The old me would have accepted that invitation backstage. But the new me is a coward.

Riley

"The tip of the neighbour's iceberg often looks very nice."

—Roy A. Ngansop

SHE KNOWS IT is a gamble, but then, what does she have to lose?

She's already lost Klein. There are only a couple of keys with the potential to unlock the door to his wanting her again. One, guilt. And two, rejection.

She's learned enough about Klein's past to know they are his Achilles heel. She sees no point in wasting energy on any efforts that will not get her what she wants. And what she wants is Klein.

She turns the leased G-Wagon onto the rural road that leads to some of Nashville's biggest mansions, the area where every home is occupied by some recognizable country music star name. She intends to live here one day herself. Klein has so far avoided buying in this section, and she knows the reason why. It's not that he can't afford it yet. He can. And then some. It's more about the fact that he doesn't see himself as one of these people.

But she considers it her personal mission to change that, to help him see himself as she sees him, as the rest of the world sees him, really.

It hasn't proven as easy as she had first imagined. And no, she hadn't anticipated the breakup. That stint in rehab had opened Klein's eyes to things he had once seen very differently.

Sometimes, she wishes he had never stopped drinking. Not for his health, of course, but she had liked the Klein who drank. He'd been fun and a little reckless, a combination that worked for her. She had fit in his life then. Sober, he saw her as a connection to all of that and a temptation he couldn't handle.

It wasn't like she'd been trying to pull him down into the dregs of alcoholism, but what was wrong with having a little fun now and then? They'd had great times together. All those nights on the road, not going to bed until the sun was about ready to come up.

The truth is she misses those days. She'd known that Klein. Known how to handle him. How to make him want the same things she wanted.

He'd been an easy sell, really. Klein had a lot of holes in his soul. Most of them came from his early beginnings. She had gotten enough out of him at times to see that he didn't remember a lot of the bad things that landed him in foster care. The scars were there nonetheless, and he had learned at some point along the way to use his songwriting and alcohol as mutual friends in his quest to permanently erase those scars.

Only, they never went away. And she supposes they never will. One thing she does know for sure. They are a lot more bearable for Klein under the haze of alcohol than they are under the stark reality of sobriety.

She glances at the GPS on her phone. Notes that she's only a couple of miles from the Ashford house. She's been invited to an industry party being held at the home of Holden Ashford and CeCe MacKenzie. The country music stars who have long been Klein's idols.

Because she works for one of the biggest labels in town, Klein's label, in fact, Riley was invited to tonight's party. She wonders if she would have been invited had Klein been in town. Knows in fact that the higher-ups would have made sure she wasn't. First and foremost, they care about keeping Klein happy. Once word of their breakup had gotten around, she'd been called into the label head's office for a not-so-covert grilling on whether she and Klein would be able to operate in the same orbit. The real question had been whether Klein would want them to fire her.

But Klein would never have asked for such a thing. If they thought so, they didn't know him very well.

Even so, Riley has no desire to push buttons that don't

need to be pushed. She had assured Sam Parker, the label head, that she was a big girl, and there would be no reason for Klein to worry about her making him uncomfortable.

Apparently, she'd turned out to be a pretty good actress because Mr. Parker had bought her version of things. She recalls now the aggravating smirk on the label head's face, as if he had known all along that a girl like Riley would never keep a catch like Klein.

She can't wait for the day she can personally hand him an invitation to her wedding to Klein. And it will happen. There is no doubt in her mind.

She presses a hand to her belly. And wonders why so many women in this world allow themselves to be told what their destiny will be by people who have decided they no longer want them.

It's really just a matter of finding the weak spot of the person you need to see things differently. And everyone has a weak spot. She knows Klein's, for sure. Knows the thing that had defined him, despite all of his success.

And that is the fact that he had not been wanted by his parents. Some might consider it cruel to let him suffer the way she knows he is suffering now.

But on some level, it seems appropriate to her. Klein has caused her suffering without a doubt. By the time she gives him what he wants, he will be so grateful to be relieved of his pain that he will have no problem forgiving her.

She's reached the driveway to the Ashford estate. A

security guard stands at the gate, ducks his head to her lowered window, and says, "Good evening. May I have your name, ma'am?"

"Riley. Riley Haverson."

He scans the list on his iPad, finds her name, taps the screen, and says, "Yes, ma'am. Go ahead. Enjoy your evening."

"Thank you so much," she says, noticing the guard's envy for her vehicle and then driving forward. She is spending nearly her last penny each month to keep up the lease on the G-Wagon, but appearances are everything. If you don't look like you can afford the world, no one is ever going to consider you worthy of having it.

In a quarter mile or so, she reaches the circular entrance to the front of the enormous house. It is lit up floor to floor, light streaming from every window. Two more security guards stand at the front door, double-checking guest names on their own lists before letting them in.

A valet walks up to her vehicle, opens the door, and greets her. "I'll park this for you, ma'am."

"Thank you," she says, unfolding her long legs and getting out. She notices the way his gaze drops to the hem of her short dress. She could mind his impertinence, but Riley never discounts evidence of her beauty in the face of men, regardless of their age or occupation. She flips her blonde hair over her shoulder and walks with complete certainty on her four-inch Prada heels to the front door.

She presses a hand to her belly, uncertain for a moment of the flowy dress she'd chosen to hide her condition. But then, she'd practically been starving herself to delay the visible evidence, and so far, it has worked. She'd read enough about pregnancy to know the baby will pull the nutrients it needs at her expense. A flash of resentment scorches through her, but then she blinks it away. This baby is her ticket, after all. Hardly makes sense to resent it.

She waits for her name to be rechecked before stepping inside the house. It's even more incredible than she had imagined, and it is all she can do to contain an audible sigh of envy. This is the life she wants. *This* is the life she's determined to have.

Raising her chin, she walks through the foyer, following the noise of conversation humming beneath the music coming from strategically placed Bose speakers. She reaches an enormous room where several large, beautiful leather sofas are scattered around, the size of the room easily handling them.

Industry faces she immediately recognizes are engaged in conversations around the room. Her gaze instantly finds Holden Ashford in the far right corner. Gorgeous, famous Holden Ashford. He's talking to Sam Parker, the label head, and they appear to be having a fairly intense conversation. She wonders for a moment if Barefoot Outlook, Holden and CeCe's band, is considering a label change.

She hopes not, simply for the prestige they bring to the label. But it would be nice to see the jackass who runs it take the blow. Holden laughs and shakes his head then, so maybe not, she decides.

A black, white, and tan dog with long legs trots into the room just then. Riley doesn't know much about dogs. She's never really cared for them, but she knows that people like people who like dogs. So she squats down and coos a hello. "You must be Hank Junior," she says, recognizing his face from the magazine articles she's read about this family. This dog is very much at the center of it. He allows himself to be petted, but his ears drop a little, and his tail stops wagging. And she wonders if he somehow knows that she doesn't usually pay any attention to his kind.

Apparently, he does, because he trots off again. She watches him go, stopping by a group of women talking. And then she sees CeCe MacKenzie-Ashford bend over and give him a hug. "Hey, there, sweetie," she says.

The dog's tail begins to wave back and forth, and she envies that dog for a moment. He's so clearly loved by CeCe, knows his place in this home. It hardly seems fair that a dog could have all that. But then she doesn't doubt her own ability to land exactly what she wants. It's just a matter of time. Klein lives in this same sphere of incredible wealth and notoriety. And one day, not too long from now, she'll belong here, too. Both of us will, she acknowledges silently, placing a hand at the center of her belly and giving it a deliberate pat.

Klein

"But, instead of what our imagination makes us suppose
and which we worthless try to discover, life gives us
something that we could hardly imagine."
—Marcel Proust

IT'S AFTER ONE A.M. when I get back to the hotel.

The doorman greets me with exuberant cheer, hotel guest protocols clearly mandating whatever the customer requires is met with complete staff approval. Including post midnight cheer.

I slip into the elevator, start to tap my room floor number, then hesitate and push another floor altogether.

I wait as it glides to a stop and opens. I step into the silent hallway, consider the wisdom in my decision, and start walking before I can talk myself out of it.

At her door, I again hesitate, then rap once, hard.

No answer.

I try again, three consecutive knocks. I hear footsteps

on the other side, sense her looking through the door's peephole.

A few seconds pass, and I am sure she's weighing the wisdom of opening the door to me. And rightly so.

But then the locks click. And the door swings in.

She's wearing one of the hotel's luxurious robes. It's pulled close against her neck and belted tight at the waist. She stares at me with wide blue eyes, eyes I've thought about at times in my life when I knew better. When she wasn't available. When I wasn't available. Her lips, deep red, full lips, are parted slightly, as if she wants to speak but doesn't know what to say.

"Hey." My voice rasps out the word, the effects of the concert still evident in my hoarseness.

"Hey," she says, surprise and a question underlining the response.

"You're still up."

"Sort of."

"Were you sleeping?"

"Ah, no," she admits.

"Jet lag?"

"Maybe."

I'd like for her to elaborate, wonder if I have anything to do with her inability to sleep. I decide I'm being arrogant, and say, "I'm still jazzed. Wanna talk?"

"Here?" she asks, throwing a hand back at the room.

"Yeah. If that's okay with you."

There's a stretch of silence while she visibly weighs her response. "Ah, sure," she says, stepping back.

I follow her in, closing the door behind me. The room is soft with lamplight.

She walks to the minibar, opens it, and says, "Would you like something to drink?"

"Water would be great."

She leans in and pulls out a bottle, handing it to me. She moves to the coffee table in the center of the room and picks up a glass. "I was actually having some wine in the hope of sleeping before dawn. Do you mind?"

"No, I'm good," I say.

"Are you sure? I don't have to have it."

"I'm not bothered by other people drinking. Really. Go ahead."

She picks up her glass and takes a seat on the sofa. "Please. Sit."

I drop onto the far end, crossing a booted foot over my knee.

"You were amazing tonight," she says.

"The crowd was great," I say, deferring her compliment.

"They were great because you were great," she says, taking a sip of her red wine.

The look of appreciation on her face makes me clear my throat and lean forward, elbows on my knees. "I'm not sure I'll ever get used to performing in front of that many people."

"You looked so comfortable up there. Like it's what you were born to do."

I laugh a little. "I'm glad it looked that way. Sometimes, I still feel as if someone is going to figure out I don't belong up there and call me on it. Report me to the imposter police or something."

She smiles and shakes her head. "If you don't belong up there, who would?"

I cock an eyebrow at her. "There are so many talented artists in Nashville. You know it's true."

"Yeah, there are," she says. "And I get the whole imposter thing. When I got songwriter of the year, I kept expecting someone to tell me it was a joke, and they were just kidding."

"Really?" Now, I'm surprised.

"Really."

"I watched the CMAs that night. I thought what you said was exactly what I would have said."

"You did?"

"Yeah. I grew up listening to country music in my foster dad's truck. He'd be delivering sawdust to farms all over South Carolina, and I would ride with him, cranking George Strait and Alan Jackson every time they came on. We'd sing along together. He had a great voice. Better than mine, actually. I've thought so many times that he should have been the one who made it in country music. Not me."

"Did he ever try?"

I shake my head. "No. He never saw himself like that. But he saw me that way."

"Did he encourage you to come to Nashville?"

"He did. In fact, he's the only reason I finally worked up the courage to catch a bus there when I did. The day I got off at the station, I spotted at least three other guys who looked just like me, fresh out of the country with stars in their eyes. Bad haircuts and all. I never thought I had anything on them."

She smiles. "That night I saw you at the Bluebird, you didn't look like you had stars in your eyes."

"I felt like a fish out of water. And then when I met you, I thought for sure I would have a panic attack performing in front of you."

"In front of me?" she asks, clearly surprised.

"Yeah. I was intimidated as hell."

"I find that hard to believe," she says.

"It's true."

She shakes her head a little. "You were incredible that night. Thirty seconds into the first song, I knew you were the next big thing."

"I sure didn't."

She hesitates, and then, "Your humility is part of your appeal."

"My foster mom used to tell me that it didn't pay to get a big head. And that if I did, God would be forced to find a way to get my feet back on the ground."

"You believe that?"

I shrug. "I don't like arrogant people. I never wanted to be one."

"Me, either," she says. And then, after a moment, "Not sure why I married one, given that."

"Josh got his share of confidence, I suppose."

"You could say that." She takes a sip of her wine, then turns her gaze direct on mine and says, "Sometimes I wonder if I ever really knew him at all. I had this feeling that there was something I didn't know. Like there was a curtain I hadn't yet managed to pull. Maybe I didn't want to know what was behind it."

I study my water bottle for a moment or two, then meet her gaze. "Do you think we ever really know another person?"

"I think we know parts of them, but I'm pretty sure everyone keeps something back. The stuff we think we'll be judged for, or we think we might be rejected for."

"But if you love someone, shouldn't you be willing to accept those things?"

"If they're acceptable. Sometimes, things aren't."

I consider this, acknowledge the truth in it. "Some things are bigger than others, though."

"True."

The lamplight is soft around her, and I let myself take her in, fully, my gaze on hers. I let her see what I'm thinking, realizing as I do that I've never let her know I find her beautiful. In the past, there's always been a reason to keep things on a professional footing: Josh, Riley, business. Tonight, I'm wondering if there's still a reason.

She looks down at her wine, blows out a soft whoosh of air. "Why are you here, Klein? In my room, I mean."

I could play off the question, make light of it, but I owe her more than that. "I'm not sure. I know why I want to be here, but I'm also pretty sure that's unwise."

"Oh, we're doing wisdom, are we?" Her gaze is direct, her smile soft.

"Not sure it's a label that applies too well to me these days."

"What have you done that was unwise?"

"Plenty."

"Run one by me."

I tilt my head against the back of the chair and study the ceiling. "It might change how you see me."

"See. There's that fear thing."

I look up then, meet her gaze head-on. "My track record with women is highly questionable."

"Why do you think that is?"

"Looking for love in all the wrong places?"

"Aren't we all?"

"Is it true Josh was having an affair?"

"Ah, yeah. It's true."

"I'm sorry."

She shakes her head. "Fool me once, shame on you. Fool me twice, shame on me."

"Not the first one then."

"Apparently."

"You didn't deserve that."

"No one deserves betrayal."

I think about this. "No."

I feel the moment awareness starts to hum. It's a tangible current that crosses the space between us, the electricity nearly a visible line in the glowy light of the room.

I can see the awareness bloom on her face, the way her eyes darken a little, her lips parting beneath a soft release of breath.

"You're heading back in the morning?" she asks, her gaze direct on mine.

"Yeah," I say, wondering for a moment if I really want to leave, if I'm ready to go back to Nashville and what has started to feel like an empty life there. What is it I'm considering?

"When are you leaving?"

"I-ah, I had planned to take a few days and see some of the countryside."

"That sounds nice."

Silence hangs between us. I stand, shoving my hands in the pockets of my jeans. "I should go. It's late."

She stands too, pulling the robe tighter and making a move toward the door. "Yeah. You'll have a flight to catch in the morning."

I walk to the door, stop, and turn to face her. "This might sound crazy, but would you mind if I went with you? Maybe just for a couple of days?"

Her surprise is evident in the ensuing silence. And then, "Ah, you mean travel together?"

I realize I've shocked her. Clearly, it was a stupid idea. "I don't know what I was thinking. I should get back to Nashville. Hadn't planned to be away longer. I'll have plenty to catch up on."

She starts to say something, stops, and then says, "No. You should come with me. I'd really like having the company."

"Really?"

"Yeah. Really."

"I don't want to impose on your plans."

"The plan was loose. Still is."

"I don't go off the calendar too often."

She smiles. "Well, maybe this is a good time to start."

Conscience tugs at me as I tick through visual reminders of the commitments on my calendar. My stomach dips a bit at the thought of blowing off names who have been important to my career. The old fear of making a choice that decimates everything I've worked for pulls at me, and

I wonder if some part of me wants to blow it all up. And I wonder if what I really do want is out.

"If you're sure," I find myself saying.

"I'm sure," she says.

We're facing each other just short of the closed door. My intention of leaving recedes from immediate reach. Instead, I'm looking at her mouth, remembering with sudden clarity how many times I've thought about what it would be like to kiss her.

I suddenly need to know.

Want sends a flare of heat through my stomach. It radiates up to my chest, and I sway an inch closer. Her eyes are open, and she's looking directly at me, as if waiting to see what my intent is.

I show her, dipping in to brush my lips against hers.

Touching her triggers the admission that I have wanted this beyond conscious memory. My logical brain shuts down and need takes over. I reach for her, my hands on her waist. She loops her arms around my neck, a soft whoosh of breath telling me she's thought about this, too. "Klein."

My name on her lips dials up the heat inside me, and I sink my mouth onto hers, kissing her full and deep while I press my body into hers, making no secret of how much I want her. We kiss like that, hot, heavy, intent, until I realize that pretty soon there won't be any turning back from where we're headed. And there's a bed a few yards away.

I pull back, looking down into her want-dazed eyes, feeling a deep and undeniable satisfaction that I have put it there. "I don't guess there would be any point in denying how much I want to stay, would there?"

"Um." She laughs a light laugh. "Probably not."

"Okay, then," I say. I run a hand through my hair, backing toward the door. "I'll be heading to my room."

She's still standing against the wall, her lips parted, moist from our kissing. "You sure?"

"I'm pretty sure you'll thank me for it in the morning."

"Hmm." In that lone syllable, I can tell she disagrees.

But I know I'm right. Whatever is going to be between Dillon and me, it isn't going to be casual. "So what time are we heading out?"

She glances at her watch. "You up for a short night?"

"At this point, yeah."

"I'll set my alarm for a few hours from now and get us a rental car."

"We're really doing this."

It's not a question, so I say, "We're really doing this."

And for the first time in longer than I want to admit, I'm looking forward to what is ahead.

Klein

"Stab the body and it heals, but injure the heart and the
wound lasts a lifetime."
—Mineko Iwasaki

I WAKE UP to the crack of light ducking in through
the hem of the hotel room's heavy curtains.

Not sure what time it is, I throw myself out of bed,
head for the bathroom and brush my teeth. I reach for my
supplement box and take this morning's allotted vitamins
with a bottle of water. I then pick up the phone in the
bedroom and order a pot of coffee from room service,
determined to wake up.

I open the curtains, blinking against the sudden
onslaught of sunlight. I crack the window, the sound of
Paris traffic humming through the opening. I'm hit
with instant memory of what had happened before I left
Dillon's room. I remember what it felt like to kiss her.
How I had wanted so much more. And then I think about

109

Riley, and guilt splashes across me like a bucket of water in the face.

I feel tarnished, as if I've done something so wrong that I don't deserve to entertain the notion of being with someone like Dillon.

I'm about to get in the shower when a wave of nausea sweeps over me. Pain stabs at both my temples, the kind of headache I used to get with a massive hangover. Only I hadn't had a thing to drink last night, so I have no idea what to attribute it to. Dehydration, maybe. Probably should have had more water after the show last night.

I think about the plans I had agreed to with Dillon and wonder now what I had been thinking. I can't leave Paris and go driving through the countryside. I need to get back to Nashville.

I've stopped the thought there because I can't find the words to finish it. Back to Nashville for what? Riley and the awful reminder of what might have been? Just the thought rolls another wave of nausea through me.

The phone next to the bed rings. I walk over and pick it up with a rusty hello.

"Hey, it's Dillon," she says, sounding far more awake and cheerful than I am.

"Morning," I say.

"Did I wake you?" she asks.

"No. I was just waiting for some coffee. I'll sound more alive once I've downed a cup or two."

She laughs softly. "So I've already been for a run in the Tuileries Garden. And I had my coffee a couple of hours ago."

"You're way ahead of me."

"Well, you are the one who worked last night," she says. "So, about today. I just want you to know you don't have to follow through on that. It was late, and—"

"Have you changed your mind about wanting me to go?"

"No, no, of course not. It's not that at all. I just didn't want you to feel obligated."

"I don't feel obligated."

"So, you do want to go?"

Now would be the moment to take the out and head back to Nashville. Try to make some sense of what I'd left behind, but that's not what I find myself saying. "I. . .yeah, I could use some downtime."

"Really? Okay. Well. That sounds great. I've been working on getting a rental car. The service actually said they can deliver it to the hotel. I thought maybe we could head out in an hour or so. Would that work?"

"Yeah," I say, "that's good with me."

~

AND IT ALL sounded great, except it doesn't really go like that. About fifteen minutes after I've finished my second cup of coffee, the pounding in my head has reached a level I can barely tolerate. And I'm seeing little pinpoints

111

of light. Every time I close my eyes, I can see them against the back of my lids.

The pain is now a full-blown ten or better. And all of a sudden, I realize I'm going to be sick. I barely make it to the bathroom before losing the coffee I just drank. My head is pounding so hard that I sink down against the bathroom wall, closing my eyes, and wondering how I'm going to get back to the bed.

I don't know how long I sit there, but it's a long time because any attempt I make to move brings on a fresh wave of nausea.

A knock sounds at the door, but I can't manage to find my voice to call out, and there's no way I can get up to answer it. I continue sitting, waiting for enough relief from the pain to be able to get up.

The phone in the bedroom rings once, twice, three times. Again, I have no idea how much time has passed, but I eventually hear a key turn in the door, and then Dillon's voice calling out, "Klein, are you in here?"

"Yeah," I call out in a weak voice. "I'm in the bathroom. I might have a migraine."

I hear a French-accented voice saying, "Please let me know if there's anything else you need, madame."

"Thank you so much," Dillon says. And then she's standing in the bathroom doorway, dropping down beside me. "Klein. What happened?"

"I'm not sure. I woke up feeling sick with a killer

headache, and then it just kind of exploded. I've never really had anything like this before."

"Let me call the front desk and see about getting a doctor to come here to see you."

"I'm not sure I need one."

"Yes, you do. You're white as that towel."

"Thanks, Dillon," I say. And then another wave of nausea hits me. I lean back and close my eyes, praying I don't throw up again.

Dillon

"The best revenge is to be unlike him who performed the injury."
—Marcus Aurelius

I CALL THE front desk and ask if there is a concierge doctor available at the hotel.

"Oui, yes, madame. Bien sûr. You have an emergency?"

"I don't think so, but if the doctor could come as soon as possible, that would be best."

"Of course, madame. I shall ring him right away. He will arrive at the room within fifteen minutes. Is this the room you wish him to come to?"

"Yes. Yes, please. Thank you so much."

I find a glass on the desk by the window and pour from a bottle of water nearby. I take it into the bathroom, sit and squat beside Klein, holding up the glass. "Here. You should drink something. Do you think you could be dehydrated?"

"I don't know. I've never really had anything like this before."

"Have you taken anything?"

"Just the supplements I take when I get up."

"And you've taken them all before?"

"Yes," he says. He presses a finger to each of his temples, grimacing.

"Can I help you get back to the bed?"

"I'm not sure I'll make it without throwing up, and I certainly wouldn't want to subject you to that," he says.

"Please. Don't think about me. This is about you and getting you feeling better."

"Can we just sit here for a few more minutes?"

"Of course," I say. I'm silent now because I feel like forcing Klein to talk is not the kind thing to do. Within a few minutes, a knock sounds at the door. I get up and open it and find a pleasant-faced, older Frenchman holding a doctor's bag standing on the other side.

"Bonjour, madame. You have called for a doctor?"

"Yes. Thank you. Thank you so much. Please come in." He follows me inside, and I lead the way to the bathroom where Klein is still sitting with his back against the wall.

"Bonjour, monsieur. How may I help you?"

"I have an excruciating headache," Klein says in a weak voice. "And nausea."

"Perhaps we can help you to the bed?"

The doctor and I both help Klein up and guide him back

to the bedroom. I stand a few feet away while the doctor checks his vitals. He pulls a digital thermometer from his bag, inserts it into a plastic sanitary sleeve, and sticks it under Klein's tongue.

He then does a series of visual tests asking Klein to identify how many fingers he's holding up. "It is possible that your headache is a migraine as you suspect. But have you ever had this headache before?"

"No. Nothing like this one."

"I have a very strong medication to give you for help with the pain. This should last several hours, but you will need to remain in bed. No driving. It is quite sedating."

Klein nods in agreement. And I can imagine that he is relieved to be given a few hours escape from the pain.

"I will write the prescription. There is a pharmacy not far from the hotel. I will communicate with the concierge, and someone will bring the medicine to your room shortly if that is okay?"

"Yes, thank you so much," Klein says.

The doctor gives us each a polite smile and leaves the room.

I sit down on the side of the bed. "Would you like me to see if I can add another day to our stay? You're not going to feel like going anywhere today."

"Yes. Please."

"Let me just call the front desk and see what I can do."

I decide to use the phone by the door so that Klein can

close his eyes and maybe sleep a little. I call the front desk and explain the situation, waiting on hold for a couple of minutes while the very nice woman assisting me checks to see if it will be possible for us to add another day to our stay. When she comes back, her tone is immediately apologetic, "I am very sorry, madame, but it will be possible only to continue another night for one of the two rooms. We are fully booked."

"Oh, okay," I say. "Does it matter which room?"

"Either one, but only the one."

"Then I will go ahead and check out of my room. If you could leave Mr. Matthews's room as it is for another day, that would be great."

"Yes, madame. I am sorry we are not able to further accommodate you."

"Thank you," I say, and hang up. When I walk back into the room, Klein is not asleep. His eyes are open, and I can see that he is still in a great deal of pain.

"I heard the conversation," he says. "There's really no reason for you to find somewhere else to stay. There's plenty of room in here if you don't mind hanging with a guy out for the count for a while."

"Oh, I'm sure you would rather be alone."

"Dillon, I don't think I'm going to know whether you're here much of the time or not, especially once I get my drugs."

I smile a little at this. And he tries to smile back, but the effort turns into a grimace.

"Are you sure?" I ask.

"Positive," he says. "And if you're not keen on sharing the bed, that sofa is a pullout."

"That will be more than sufficient for me, and anyway, I'll be happy to hang around and be your nurse."

He laughs a little at this, but then says, "Oh, dang, that hurt."

"Here, no more laughing, you need to rest. And as soon as someone comes with your medicine, I'm going to leave you alone for a bit."

The knock at the door surprises me. I can't imagine they've gotten here that quickly with the medication. But when I open the door, a young man in a dark suit says, "Your order from the pharmacy, madame."

"Yes, thank you so much."

He nods his head and turns for the elevator. I close the door, take the bottle of pills out of the bag, and go into the bathroom to get a glass of water. I remove the top, read the directions, and see that he is to take one tablet.

I hand it to him along with a glass of water, and he takes it gratefully.

"Thank you," he says, lying back on the pillow and closing his eyes. "I appreciate your help more than I can say."

"I'm going to let you get some sleep, and I'll go finish checking out of my room."

"There's a key to this room on the desk there. Take that with you."

"Thank you. Would you like me to close this curtain and make it darker?"

"That would be great," he says. I pull all of the curtains a little tighter, blocking out as much light as possible, and then head for the door.

"I'll be back to check on you in a bit."

"Thank you, Dillon." And I can already hear the medication taking its effect in his voice.

~

I GO BACK to my room. I have to be checked out within an hour. I take my suitcase downstairs and ask the concierge if I might store it for a bit. Once I've settled up at the front desk with my bill, I decide to take my laptop and get a cup of coffee in the bar. I ask for a table, a booth in the corner. A smiling, pretty young waitress brings the coffee to me a few minutes later in a silver pot with a white porcelain cup.

"Thank you so much," I say.

"Please do enjoy," she says and then leaves me to it.

I open my laptop, type in the password, and pour myself a cup of the steaming brew, taking a sip. It is delicious. I take another sip and then open my email account. I'm expecting a blast from Josh, but surprisingly, I don't see anything from him. My gaze snags on an address I don't recognize. I consider ignoring it as I do most junk mail, but something about the name has me tapping and opening it.

At the top of the email is a photo of me ducking into the rehearsal hall yesterday afternoon with Klein. I'm surprised by the picture since I hadn't noticed anyone around. There might've been a photographer or even a regular person snapping a photo of Klein. And then I wonder who sent this. I glance back at the email address. Riley.countrymusicforever. And then I realize it's Klein's ex.

I wonder what her motive could possibly be for sending me this. I can't imagine that it's just a nice gesture. But would she be jealous? And why would she send it without saying anything? I scroll back up, look at the photo of Klein and me. Whoever had taken it had captured us in a moment of laughter, my head thrown back a little, a smile on my face. Klein is looking down at me with a half-grin on that incredibly good-looking face of his.

Something about this definitely isn't right. I consider replying with a question mark but decide against it. Whatever issues Riley has with Klein, she'll have to take up with him. I close out the email. But curiosity prevails, and without letting myself change my mind, I type her name into the Google search bar. The first thing that pops up is an article about Riley and Klein, dated almost a year ago.

There's a photo of the two of them dancing at a club in Nashville.

He's holding her tight against him, and she's looking up into his face with utter adoration. I click on a link that takes me to the original article. I read the gossip magazine's interpretation of the then hot new relationship between Riley and Klein. I glance back at the photo, see that he looks more than a little intoxicated.

Pre-rehab, I assume.

I look closer at Riley's face and see that she had also been extremely inebriated. I wonder who influenced whom. I go back to my original search and click on her Instagram account. It's not private, so I scroll through an abundance of photos. Mostly shots of Riley in different locations, different outfits. A dozen or so are photos of her with Klein, of Klein alone. The last one she had posted of him was almost three months ago. Is that when they had broken up?

I wonder who broke it off, Klein or Riley. Given the photo I just received, my guess would be Klein. I look back at the top two pictures on the Instagram page. She's certainly beautiful. And they're quite a match.

I click out of Instagram, go back to the search page again, and scroll through the first listing. I then click over to the second page for older references to Riley. There's a Tumblr account created four years ago. Curious, I tap and find a stream of beautiful photographs, all apparently taken by Riley.

Among the photos are a few of her with Aaron Rutgers. He'd been a promising young guitar player whom I'd met on a couple of occasions with Josh. I hadn't known he and Riley were ever a thing. The date on the entries indicates they'd been posted a year or so before his death.

I glance closer at one of the photos, and then it hits me that Aaron had looked remarkably like Klein. In fact, the two could have been brothers.

I sit back and consider this, something about it sending off a ping inside me. Maybe Riley was just extremely consistent with her taste in men. But somehow, I have a feeling there is more to Riley than is immediately apparent.

Riley

"A weed is but an unloved flower."
—Ella Wheeler Wilcox

I'M PRETTY SURE I was a success at the party.

I woke up early this morning thinking of how amazing it had been, how brilliant I had been in my well-planned efforts to make anyone I encountered last night like me and want to know me better. I admit it isn't something that comes naturally to me. I prefer to talk about myself. I find myself more interesting, and I'm not sure why there's anything really wrong with that, but apparently, that is not the thing that makes people want to be around you.

It was actually a bandmate of Klein's who found the nerve to share this point of view with me. One late night on the tour bus when Klein had already gone to sleep.

It was Pete Collins, one of the guitar players who had his eye on me whenever he thought Klein wasn't looking. I don't know whether Klein had noticed or not, but I certainly had. Not that it bothered me. I found such information useful and would have used it against him, had I ever felt the need to do so. That night he had poured himself several shots of liquid courage before joining me on the sofa at the front of the bus. I'd been sitting on one end, and he lowered himself down next to me. Way too close.

But I pretended to be interested, curious to see where this would lead. Pete got to his point without much preamble, putting his hand on my knee and giving it a squeeze.

"So, it looks like you and I are the only ones awake. It seems like we could find something interesting to do."

"You think?" I asked, tilting my head and giving him a look of innocence.

"I can think of a few possibilities we might get around to." He lifts his shoulders, unconcerned. "He's asleep. He's had a few."

"You mean like you have?" I asked.

"I can handle my liquor."

"That remains to be seen," I said.

He studied me for a long moment and then said, "You think no one has you figured out."

"You think you do?"

"Oh, I know I do. You're planning on getting a ring from Klein, and there's not much you won't do to make sure that happens."

"I'm not going to deny that I want a future with him. Why would I deny that?"

"The question is, does he want a future with you." The words struck their intended sweet spot, and I gave him a deliberately neutral smile.

"It seems like you have some idea of why he would want that."

"Yeah, no doubt. I'd like to know what you'll be giving him when you go back there in a bit and slip in bed next to him."

"You know he would fire you if I breathed a word of this, right?"

"Right," he agreed, "but I also know he would dump you if I breathed a word of the mess you made of Aaron Rutgers's life when he decided he didn't want to make you a permanent thing."

I felt the heat rising from the center of my chest, flaming my face. Even as I tried to tamp it back, I wasn't willing to let him see that he had gotten to me.

"What do you know about it?" I asked in a deliberately smooth voice.

"Enough," he said.

I could see by the look on his face that he did indeed know more than I was comfortable with him revealing at the moment. So, I changed course. Used the one foolproof weapon that had never failed me. I put my hand on his thigh and rubbed my palm back and forth across his jeans.

"Nothing is going to happen here tonight, Pete. Are we clear?"

"Yeah," he said, waiting.

"You have my number. When we get back to Nashville, give me a call."

He stood, looking down at me with a satisfied smile on his face. "Oh, I will, Riley. I will be giving you a call." And with that, he headed for his bunk at the back of the bus.

I had barely gotten through the front door of my apartment once we were back in Nashville before the phone rang, and Pete's number flashed across the screen. I considered not answering, but I fully believed Pete when he said he wouldn't hesitate to share what he knew with Klein. I declined the call, sent him an abrupt text: **Be here in one hour or don't come at all.**

The knock at the door announced him as right on time. No surprise to me. I pushed back a surge of irritation, telling myself there was this and nothing more. I opened the door to a grinning Pete, barely able to conceal his obvious interpretation of victory. I waved him in. "You didn't waste any time, did you?"

"I've never been one to ignore opportunity when it presents itself."

"There are other words for that," I said. "Blackmail. I'm pretty sure that's illegal."

"So why did you invite me over here?"

"We both know why I invited you."

"And I'm a man of my word. You keep your part of the deal. I'll keep my part of the deal. Klein's not ever going to hear from me what went on with you and Aaron."

"Might I ask how you know?"

"Believe it or not, we found ourselves in the same waiting room of the counselor I see. Aaron was pretty messed up."

"I think his state of mind is strictly his responsibility. I had nothing to do with it."

He gave me a long questioning look. "Is that how you really see it?"

I lifted my shoulders in a nonchalant shrug. "Aaron was a grown man. He made his own choices, decisions, and those led to a certain outcome."

"An outcome you helped create," he said.

"Might I ask why you care so much about Aaron?"

"He's a friend from way back, and I hated seeing him torn up the way he was."

"Oh, you hated it so much that you're using what you know about it to go to bed with me and keep it from the guy who's given you your best gig to date. Am I warm?"

He didn't even bother to look ashamed, and I recognized in him something I knew to be accurate about myself. Other people liked to deny the fact that self came first. We were all taught the golden rule growing up that we should do unto others as we would have done unto us, but what I know to be true, and I am now sure Pete actually lived by, was the fact that the other people were just kidding themselves. We all live for self.

Wasn't it the rare person who would actually step aside and wait for the other people in the burning movie theater to get out first? Wasn't it far more likely that most people would step over anyone in the way to keep the flames from consuming them?

My analogy wasn't far off in comparison to Pete using what he knew about me. He would be literally burning my life down, the life I had recently redesigned for myself, and I wasn't about to give up.

"Enough talk," I said. "Let's get on with things."

"Hmm, romance, I like it," Pete said.

"You do know you're pushing your luck, right?"

He chuckled softly. "I'm guessing, yes. So, one night with you here and now, and you will never hear from my lips another word about anything other than my sincerest best wishes for you and Klein and your glowing happy future, babies and all."

"Shut up," I said and lifted my face to his.

It was two A.M. when I woke up and all but rolled Pete out of my bed. Spending the night was not part of the deal. "Please, go, now," I said.

He stumbled to his feet, shaking himself awake and saying, "I'd be offended, but judging from your response a couple of hours ago, I don't think I'm being kicked out for lack of performance."

"You really are an arrogant bastard, aren't you?"

"Just stating the facts, ma'am," he said, pulling on his jeans and shrugging into his sweater. "I know I thoroughly enjoyed myself, and it's not that I wouldn't have guessed as much, but I can certainly see why Klein lets you hang around."

"You're disgusting. Get out."

"All right, all right," he said, grabbing his shoes and backing out of the room. "The pleasure was all mine, ma'am, and a little of yours, too."

I pulled a book off my nightstand and hurled it at the doorway, but he'd closed the door behind him, and the hardback landed with a solid thud against the wood.

I barely suppressed a scream, pressing my lips together and arching my back until I heard the apartment door open and close. I hated letting anyone get the best of me.

If Pete had really had any idea what I'm capable of, he would never have come to my apartment that night. I picture the stack of pillboxes Klein uses to dole out his daily supplements. Since his stint in rehab, he takes a ton of different things, having bought into his doctor's recommendations for attempting to undo some of the damage his heavy drinking did to his nutrient status over the last few years.

When Klein sets his mind to something, no one is more disciplined or dedicated than he is. This handy bit of knowledge served me well in coming up with my retribution plan. He doesn't know I still have the key to his place. He'd actually never given me one. I'd lifted a spare from his kitchen drawer, taken it to the hardware store one morning while Klein was still sleeping and had a copy made.

I'd always believed in planning for the unexpected. But somehow, even though I had not anticipated Klein ending things with us, I always liked to have money in the bank where options were concerned. Having a key to Klein's house had undoubtedly given me options.

He keeps two weeks' worth of supplements in dosing containers at a time to prevent having to redo them so often. That had given me fourteen days to play with, and when I'd learned of his trip to Paris, I slipped into his house one afternoon, planting my little concoction as something to take along with him. It had been so easy, really. I'd simply opened a few of the capsules with ingredients indiscernible from the color of what I was replacing it with.

He would discover the first surprise on day three of his trip. I'd taken pity on him, deliberately waiting, avoiding the day of his concert. No point in depriving all of those people who paid to see him on their night out. My timeframe was generous, I thought. A few little punishments doled out within the two weeks. Plenty of time for Klein to change his mind about us. And if he doesn't, my last pillbox surprise will be something very different from the killer headache he is likely to experience with the kinder examples of my efforts.

Dillon

"At sunrise, everything is luminous but not clear."

—Norman Maclean

I GO BACK to the room at two o'clock, taking my suitcase with me. I let myself in quietly, tiptoeing across the rug-covered floor, to the side of the bed, where I see Klein staring up at me, his eyes open.

"Hey," I say, "how are you feeling?"

"The headache's gone," he says, cautiously, as if he's afraid it will roar back at any moment.

"Wonderful," I say. "I'm so glad. Can I get you anything?"

"Actually," he says, his voice sleep-roughened, "I'm starving."

"Would you like me to order something from room service?"

"That would be great," he says.

"Let me look for the menu," I say, getting up to

rummage around the desk, and then finding it in the middle drawer.

"You can open those curtains if you don't mind," he says.

I pull them wide, letting afternoon sunlight into the room, and then take the menu over to the bed.

"Just let me know what you want, and I'll call it in."

He slides up to sit against the pillows. "Thanks, Dillon. I really appreciate all of this. It's way beyond the call of duty."

"I'm just sorry it happened. Have you ever had anything like this before?"

He shakes his head. "That's the weird thing. Nothing remotely like that, that wasn't self-induced, anyway." He closes the menu and adds, "I think maybe just the soup and some bread. I'm a little afraid to be too adventurous at this point."

"Sure. Something to drink?"

"A bottle of cold water would be nice."

"Okay, got it." I go over to the desk, pick up the phone, and place the order with room service. "She says it should be here in twenty minutes."

"I think maybe I'll take a shower before the food gets here. I feel like the walking dead."

"I can leave the room if you'd like."

"No, Dillon. I'm cool with it. Really."

"You know," I say, "I can find another room for tonight."

"Absolutely not," he says. "I'm the one who's put you in this position, and it's not like I need this huge room for myself anyway. Just make yourself comfortable. I'll be right back."

I turn my head as he gets out of the bed and walks to the bathroom, aware that he's in boxers and no shirt. I do catch a glimpse of his broad-shouldered back as he steps into the bathroom, and I feel a wave of heat sweep up my neck. As a distraction, I pick up my phone, drop onto a chair by the window, and scroll through my Instagram feed until bored.

I drop the phone on my lap and stare out the window. I'm in Paris, in a beautiful hotel, a country music star on the other side of the bathroom door. Surely, I can find something more relevant than staring at social media.

I head for the desk again, looking for some paper and a pen. A couple of lines had played through my head earlier. I'd meant to put them in the notes on my phone at the time but had gotten distracted and forgotten.

I close my eyes and try to remember the first line, scribbling it down as the words come to me. I wait a few moments, recalling the next line, and writing it down as well. I tap my fingers on the side of the chair. Once I've found the melody, I add the words.

"That sounds great," Klein says, startling me.

I look up with a self-conscious smile. "Oh, yeah, I was just messing with some thoughts I'd had earlier."

"It sounds great, really."

"We'll see if I can make something of it," I say.

A knock sounds at the door. Klein goes to answer it, now dressed in jeans and an untucked, long-sleeve, blue shirt. A polite waiter brings the tray into the room, sets it on the corner of the bed at Klein's indication. Klein gives him a tip, thanks him, and with a nod, the waiter leaves the room.

"That smells great," I say.

"Yeah, I'm suddenly starving. Would you like some?"

"No, I'm good. I had lunch earlier."

He carries the tray to the desk and sits down, taking the lid off the soup, and then quickly digging in.

"Mmm," he says. "That's amazing. I feel guilty about eating in front of you though."

"You shouldn't. I indulged myself earlier."

"I'm sorry. I've pretty much messed up the day."

"Don't be," I say. "It's not as if you could help it."

"Yeah, I know this is going to sound weird, but it almost felt like I'd been poisoned."

"Do you think it could have been food poisoning?"

He shrugs, lifting his shoulders. "I don't know. Maybe. I've had food poisoning before, and somehow it didn't really feel like that. I guess there are different degrees of food poisoning. Maybe this one was much more severe. Anyway, I feel like I owe you some time out of this room."

"I'm okay to stay here. You're probably weak. I can't imagine you would feel like doing much of anything."

"I feel remarkably better," he says. "We could at least go for a walk."

"I'd like that. There's a park, a block or so away, that's really nice for walking around and taking in the sights."

"That sounds good," he says, putting the lid on his soup bowl and pushing back from the desk. "I could use some fresh air, anyway. Let's head out."

Klein

"Vengeance in bloom shone in her eyes and smiled on her lips."

—Alexandre Dumas

IT ACTUALLY FEELS great to be out in the fresh air. We walk to the Jardin des Tuileries, a long block or so from the hotel. The sun is sinking, but it's warm outside, and the park is full of people, all strolling and talking. There are a couple of large fountains around which people sit in chairs.

"They seem to approach life a little differently here," I say as we pass one of the fountain areas.

"For a city that could legitimately be compared to New York," Dillon says, "it does have a different feel. It's not as hectic, frenzied."

"I was expecting a French version of New York, I guess."

"New York is a little fast for me. I get the appeal. It's

kind of like being at a party twenty-four hours a day. I just don't think I have the energy to live that. Nashville's way more my speed."

We walk in silence for a minute or so, and I can tell there's something Dillon wants to say, so I wait, giving her the time she needs to voice it.

"So, I got an email from Riley."

This surprises me. I stop, pull back, and say, "What?"

"Apparently, she saw a photo that some paparazzi had taken of us going into the rehearsal building yesterday."

"What did she say?"

"It was just the photo in the email. Nothing else. It seemed a little odd."

"It is."

"Is she the jealous type?"

"It wouldn't really matter," I say. "We're not together anymore."

"What happened there?" She presses her lips together and then says, "I'm sorry. It's none of my business. I shouldn't have asked."

"No, it's fine, really." I blow out a sigh, tip my head back and look up at the sky for a few seconds. "I broke up with Riley because it just didn't seem like we were going to be a good fit for each other. A couple of weeks after that, she sent me a text saying that she had discovered she was pregnant. She didn't keep the baby."

Dillon stops, turning to look at me with wide, horrified eyes. "You mean—"

"Yeah," I say, my voice thickening around the word, and then I swallow hard to push back the knot of emotion hanging there.

"So you didn't know until—?"

"No, I didn't."

"Oh. Klein. I'm so sorry."

I glance down at the ground, kick my toe in the soft, sandy dirt that is the footing of the garden. "I would've liked to have known, to have some role in the decision."

"I can't imagine that she wouldn't let you do that."

I'm quiet for a few seconds, weighing my words. "It would be easy for me to blame her, but in truth, I did break up with her. I put her in that position, so really, I guess it's my fault."

"You had every right to know about the baby, to be given a chance to work something out between the two of you."

"She wanted to get back together, tried to convince me. I mean, she didn't tell me about the baby, but I guess she thought if I didn't want her, for just her, then maybe it wouldn't be a good idea for the two of us to have a baby together."

"I'm so sorry."

"Our innocent baby shouldn't be the one to pay the

price for our inability to work things out." I look at Dillon then, and there are tears in her eyes.

We walk in silence for a few minutes. At some point along the way, Dillon hooks her arm through mine, and I welcome the connection to someone who feels empathy for what I have felt, who clearly understands the loss.

"It's not right," Dillon finally says, as we approach the end of the garden. "You should have had a say, Klein."

We turn and head back the way we came. I squeeze her hand against my arm but find I can't say anything that won't reveal just how broken I am.

~

WE'VE WALKED FOR a good while in silence when Dillon says, "Do you ever wonder why human beings have to hurt one another the way we do? So much of it is just unnecessary. It's not as if we feel good after we hurt someone we care about. I mean, I can't imagine that Riley did not regret what she did. Did she really need to hurt you that much?"

"I don't know. Sometimes I think it's so crazy, how we can meet someone and see in them things we think we want and find so appealing, and then at some point down the road, sometimes not even very far down the road, we see them in a completely different way. And what we had once called love, we realize, isn't that at all."

"It is crazy, isn't it?"

"We have blinders on when we first meet someone, and

all we're seeing is that immediate, I don't know, physical attraction, I guess. We all show the very best parts of ourselves to people when we first meet them and cover up the less appealing parts."

"True," I say.

"So maybe," Dillon says, "what we should be doing is giving very little credit to what we see initially, because the good is not that good, and the bad can be really bad."

"I've often thought that it's kind of funny how we go to school for twelve years growing up, to learn all the things we learned in elementary school and high school. And I wonder if we would be far better served to learn about life skills, like how to find a person who really will love you the rest of your life, for better and for worse."

"I think I would've gotten a lot more out of that," Dillon says, "than I got out of chemistry, for sure. But then again, when it comes to love, or what we think is love, do any of us ever really listen anyway?"

"Probably not," I say.

"My mom," Dillon says, "tried to teach me the red flags she said I should never ignore in a man."

"Oh, yeah? Like what?"

"Let's see," she says. "A good man can always say he's sorry. So, if I found myself with someone who could never apologize, I should cross him off the list of possibilities."

"I'll agree with that one. I would say we all need to be

able to admit we're wrong when we're wrong. What else?"

"Never accept a man who talks down to you. Like, 'If you'd work out, you'd look a lot better.' Oh, and she also said that when a good man loves you, you'll have a certain glow about you."

I smile at this. "I kind of think that's true. And it works both ways. I mean, should we really want to spend our life with someone who doesn't make us happy?"

"The thing is," Dillon says, "I don't think there's any way that we can be happy, one hundred percent of the time. Do you?"

"I think we could be happier a lot more than we are," I say. "But, on the other hand, I don't think we can look to another person for our happiness."

"There is one other thing my mama used to say," Dillon says.

"What's that?"

"That we have to figure out how to make our own self happy, and that whoever we let into our lives should add to it, make it better, bigger, greater. And they shouldn't want to change who we are. If the person we let in doesn't pretty much want to keep us exactly as we are, then they don't have any business being there."

"Did Josh fit that?" I ask.

"As it turns out," she says on a sigh, "no."

"Did you figure that out before or after you married him?"

"In hindsight, before I married him. It's just, I couldn't bring myself to admit it, because I thought I had found my true soulmate."

"What made you think that about him?"

"Truthfully?"

"Yeah."

"I guess because he liked my songs. He thought I wrote amazing songs."

"Well, you do."

"I think, on a good day, I've done all right, but back then, I didn't know that. I guess I was just starving for someone to validate my worth as a songwriter, and that's exactly what Josh did."

"And you thought you had to marry him for that?"

"No. I thought I was in love with him for that."

"Do you think now that you never loved him?"

"I can't say that. Josh has good qualities. It's just, he didn't take the part where we're faithful to each other to heart, and I guess I did."

"Do you think people are capable of that for an entire lifetime?" I ask.

"Yeah, I do. I really do. When you find the right person, the one who fills you up to the point that you have no hunger, no need to look to anyone else for the things love gives you."

"I'm pretty sure Josh is going to regret—"

"I don't think so," she interrupts.

"He should," I say.

"Thanks."

The weight in her voice tells me it is something she needs to hear.

I'm not really sure how long we've been walking, but the light has started to fade, and streetlights along the edge of the park have started to flicker on. "I have an idea," I say.

"What?"

"Why don't we get room service tonight and write a song together?"

She looks completely surprised by the suggestion, as if it is not something she would ever have imagined me wanting to do with her.

"Really?"

"Yeah, really."

"That sounds amazing," she says. "I would love to write a song with you."

"Then let's do it."

Dillon

"If music be the food of love, play on."
—**William Shakespeare**

IT'S A LITTLE awkward sharing a room with Klein. I mean, there's the whole bathroom thing and working out who's going to take a shower first. I bridge the subject as soon as we get back to the room, not wanting to delay the awkwardness.

"I could take a shower at the spa," I say. "That would probably make things a lot more—"

Klein turns in the doorway to look at me. "You should use the shower here. I can go downstairs, have a coffee, or something."

"You don't need to do that. But do you mind if I go ahead and take one?"

"No, of course, not."

I open my suitcase where I've left it on one of the luggage stands, rummage through for some clean clothes, and grab my makeup bag to take with me. Once I'm in the bathroom with the door closed and locked, I stare at myself in the mirror, noting the pink in my cheeks. I wonder if I could have sounded any more ridiculous. I tell myself to get a grip and then stand under the shower for a good ten minutes, mainly because I dread going back out into the bedroom and facing Klein. But once I've dried my hair and put on a little makeup, I have no more excuses to delay.

"We could order some dinner," Klein says, looking up from his seat at the desk. A laptop sits in front of him, and he closes the lid, standing. "I'm actually hungry."

"That sounds good," I say.

He hands me the menu, and I spend a couple of minutes perusing the options. He offers me a piece of paper and pen to write it down and says, "I'll order if you like."

"Okay." Apparently, he's already looked at the menu because as soon as I'm done, he picks up the phone and calls room service, placing the order in a polite, even voice.

When he hangs up, we stand for a moment, uneasy, until he says, "So, about that song. You still up for working on something with me?"

"Yes, I would love that."

He walks to the closet and pulls out his guitar, bringing it over to the bed and opening the case to pull it out. "Anything in particular you want to write about?" I ask.

"I kind of liked what you were working on earlier," he says.

"Really?"

"Yeah." He sits down on the corner of the bed, strums a few chords, and then picks up the melody I had tapped out earlier. I feel a little thrill of pleasure, knowing that he had paid attention enough to recall exactly what I had put down.

And then he adds, "This is what's been playing through my head ever since I heard you this morning."

He starts over, strumming my original melody, and then segues into some additional of his own.

I listen in amazement that he has added something I'm not sure I would have created myself, but I can hear that his choice is wonderful. "I can certainly understand where you get your guitar genius reputation from."

"I just try to hear it in my head before I ever pick up the guitar, and you gave me the advantage this morning of creating a beautiful start."

"Thanks," I say.

"What were your lyrics, again?" he asks.

I reach for my backpack, starting to pull the notebook out with the paper I had written them on when he says, "No, how about you sing it?"

"Ah, I don't really sing in front of other people."

"Oh, come on, let me hear it." I swallow hard, put the backpack down, and close my eyes, searching for the words. I remember the melody and then turn my back to him, facing the window and the courtyard below. I sing

147

the words softly but manage to get it done. I hold my breath a little until he says, "That was beautiful. Sing it again."

I turn around and look at him. "Again?"

"Yeah, please."

I draw in another deep breath and start to turn away when he adds, "And look at me, please."

I stand for a few moments, my voice frozen in my throat. When I start again, my voice cracks a bit, and then I close my eyes, letting the words come out as if I were alone in my office at home working on a song with no one there to hear me singing. When I'm done, Klein sits there on the edge of the bed staring at me for several long seconds.

"You have a beautiful voice, Dillon."

"Ah, no. That's not my gift. The words, if I have a gift, they would be it."

"Your voice is a gift, too. Can I ask why you didn't go for your own solo career?"

I laugh a short laugh and then, "There are some things you learn along the way that you're just not meant to do."

"I can't imagine what would have happened to make you think that."

"I actually came to Nashville intending to try to make it on my own."

"So, what happened?" he asks.

"When I first started meeting with Josh and playing my songs for him, he loved the songs themselves, but he thought I would have a hard time competing with the other female artists who were currently on their way up."

"With your voice and songwriting talent, why on earth would he have thought that?"

"I guess it was his professional opinion," I say.

"Hmm. Sounds to me like there was something else affecting his decision-making."

"Like what?"

"Maybe he didn't want you to outshine him," Klein says.

"Josh is successful and was when I met him."

"So there wouldn't be any logic in what I say. But it does make me wonder because when I hear you sing, and I know what kind of songs you write, it's only logical to me that you would have performed many of them yourself."

"It's nice to hear. I can't deny that, but I think my own lack of self-confidence is why I decided not to pursue a career as an artist. I don't think I have what it takes to get up in front of audiences the way you do. I'm too self-critical, too self-aware. I think it's worked for me to hide behind the pen, write the songs, and let someone else perform them."

"Well, there's nothing wrong with that," Klein says. "You've made an incredible career for yourself, but you know, it's not too late to try the other part of it, too."

"It's too late for me. The female artists these days are getting younger and younger, and I'm getting older."

"I can see I'm not going to change your mind about this, but you should think about it, really."

I laugh a little and shake my head. "Let's get back to the song we were working on. I think we've got something going here."

"I agree," he says, strumming out the chords again. He then starts over, singing the words from the beginning. The sound of his voice over the words I had written gives me a thrill I can't deny. It never gets old, this part, creating something that gets put to music with a beautiful voice delivering it.

As the guitar chords fade into silence, the next line comes to me. I say it out loud. Klein looks up, nods once in agreement, and starts over, adding the line at the end. He throws out the next line, and it's perfect, better, I think than I would have come up with myself. We keep at it until we've got the first verse and part of the chorus. I'm so excited I feel like a little girl at Christmas, anxious to unwrap the next present under the tree and see what it is.

The knock at the door interrupts us. A polite young woman rolls the cart into the room and opens up the side doors to pull out our plates and set them on top of the table. Once she's done, Klein signs the check, gives her a tip, and she leaves the room, wishing us a good evening.

"This smells so good," I say.

"It does," he agrees.

We pull a chair up to the table and start eating, silent for a few moments as we indulge our hunger.

"Oh my gosh," I say. "Could this be any more delicious?"

"They pretty much make every dish a work of art."

My salad is exactly that, simple, with greens, shredded carrot, and cherry tomatoes. The dressing is simple as well, a lemon and olive oil vinaigrette, but it is absolutely wonderful. "I could eat five of these," I say.

Klein smiles. "We can order more if you like."

"This is plenty, but it is just so good."

We take our time with the meal, mostly eating in silence, but it's not awkward or uncomfortable. I have to admit I find this surprising, given that I've never spent this much time alone with Klein, and he is for sure the most drop-dead gorgeous man I've ever known. And while I would expect that to make me tongue-tied and awkward, it doesn't with him.

"You're easy to be around," I say.

He looks up, putting his fork on his plate and smiling. "You sound surprised by that."

"Well, to be honest, I guess I am a little surprised."

"Why is that?"

I decide to be completely honest. "You're a big star, and you have women falling all over you all the time."

He laughs a little. "Not exactly. Sometimes, I think it was a lot easier when I wasn't well-known."

"Why?"

"People are more reluctant to approach you. There's this thing that they think you'll rebuff them, and I guess no one wants to experience rejection. It's not really like that, though," he says. "I actually like it when people come up to me and tell me what they think about my music or what they'd like to hear me do next. It's a lonelier life once you get famous."

"I guess I'm not too surprised by that," I say. "In a way, it seems like you have kind of everything at your fingertips and people wanting to do things for you, get in your good graces. But at the same time, I'm sure it's like you said. People are intimidated by fame and what all they think it includes."

"The thing is," Klein says, "you're the same person as you were before. Nothing has changed really, except making a lot more money and finally achieving your dream."

"That's a lot," I say.

"It is. Don't get me wrong. It doesn't change who you are, though. It doesn't take away the insecurities and doubts that plague you before you're famous. It seems like they would all just be washed away, but they aren't. I think it's a little disappointing to people sometimes, actually, when they're around me long enough to see some of the mystery disappear."

"Was that how it was with Riley?" I ask.

He's quiet for a few moments, and then he says, "No. She has all these ideas in her head about the ladder of success and the things you should be doing along the way, the house, the neighborhood, the kind of car you should be driving."

"And that didn't work for you?"

"No, not really. I mean, who doesn't enjoy the finer things in life? I have the ability now to have a lot of them. I'm grateful for that, but as far as obtaining stuff to mark my success on the way, no, that's never really been me, and I don't see it being me. It's not things," he says, "that are going to make a person happy. Comforts, yeah. I like comfort as well as the next guy, but what's given me the most happiness so far about whatever financial success I've obtained is giving some of it back, especially to the community where I grew up."

"I read about what you've been doing for the foster care program back home. It has to mean so much to those children."

Klein shrugs. "I was one of them. I know what it's like to reach the point where you no longer unpack your suitcase because it's pretty much a given that you won't be staying long."

My heart clenches at this instant image of a little boy arriving at another home, sure he won't be staying. "That's awful."

"My last foster family was a different story. I didn't

get there until I was fourteen, but I stayed there until I graduated from high school. They were what you would look for in a foster family, not just in it for the money. They truly tried to make the kids they took in feel like they were finally home."

"They sound like great people."

"They are. As I mentioned, my foster dad drove a sawdust truck. I would go with him sometimes. He had a big hound dog named Charles who would go with us and ride in the middle of the seat. We had stops along the way where we would pull over at a convenient spot, and I'd have to run in and get Charles his favorite snack, bacon biscuit, a slice of pumpkin pie."

I laugh. "Charles was living the high life."

"He really was," Klein says, smiling. "He was a great dog. He died right after I turned eighteen, and I didn't think my dad would survive it. He loved him that much."

"Do you ever see your foster parents?"

"I do," Klein says. "I go back as often as I can, mostly holidays and stuff. I did buy them a new house, so they have a lot more room for the kids they take in. There's a pool in the backyard and a basketball court."

"That's amazing," I say.

"Not really. I would never be able to pay them back an amount of money to show exactly how much I appreciate what they did for me. I can't even explain what it felt like when I began to realize theirs was a home I might stay in, that they actually wanted me to stay. And then for a long time, I felt guilty about that because I knew so many other kids who got bounced from place to place and never, before they were eighteen, had the chance to put down roots anywhere."

"I guess I never really thought about how incredible and meaningful fostering children really is. It is amazing to think about how easy it would be to give a child a completely different life."

"My foster family probably wouldn't call me easy, but they stuck with me when I acted out, tried to get them to send me back because I knew it was going to happen anyway."

"I'm sorry, Klein. That's not what childhood is supposed to be."

"No," he says, "but I'm grateful that the last part of it was completely different from the beginning."

"What happened to your parents? Or, wait, you don't have to answer that."

"It is what it is. They were both into drugs."

"What kind of drugs?" I ask, admittedly stunned to think this had been his beginnings.

"Heroin, actually. Not what you picture in rural South Carolina, but they both got started on heavy-duty pain medications for different reasons. When they could no longer get prescriptions for those, heroin was the next best thing, I guess."

I really don't know what to say. I start to respond and then stop.

"I know, it's out there, isn't it? You don't need to feel sorry for me, Dillon. It's not like that anymore. I kind of look at it these days as it's made me who I am and given me the incentive to try to do some good things in this world. Maybe if I hadn't gone through all of that, I would not see life that way and just be a miserable waste of time on this earth."

"You're anything but that," I say.

We finish our meal, mostly in silence, and once we've put everything back on the cart and rolled it out into the hallway, I say what it is I've been thinking about. "I want to finish the song we started tonight, but I have an idea for another one. If you don't mind, I'd like to work on that for a bit, see what comes of it. It's something you said that gave me the idea."

"Okay." We're back in the bedroom now, and he's picking up his guitar. "Got a title?"

"Roots," I say.

He looks up at me, smiles an appreciative smile, and says, "Let's hear what you've got."

Klein

"A person who never made a mistake never tried anything
new."
—Albert Einstein

AS IT TURNS out, we write until almost three in the
morning. We take a break at eleven to order a pot of
coffee from room service. I'm not sure I even need it to
stay awake because I'm so cranked by the creative process
of working with Dillon. I have a feeling the song is going
to be the one that tells my story more than anything I've
ever written myself.

I've co-written with plenty of other writers in
Nashville, so this isn't a first for me. But somehow it's
different. It's like I don't mind revealing parts of myself to
her that I would be reluctant to share with a stranger,
someone I didn't know before we walked into the writing
session together. With Dillon, it's like I'm writing with an
old friend. Someone I've known the majority of my

life. Someone who knows the shadows and fractures and ugly parts, as well as what's come since.

But I haven't known Dillon all my life. We've actually spent very little time together in the big picture of things, and yet I'm comfortable with her. I have the feeling that she accepts me for who I am and not just the shiny, polished up Nashville country music star version.

I glance at my phone at 2:52 A.M., noting the moment when it feels like the song is completely finished. I sit back in my chair and put my guitar on the floor. "I'm pretty sure I've never written anything this good."

Dillon smiles, and her face is lit with the same kind of happiness I'm feeling right at the moment. "It's amazing, isn't it," she says, "when something comes together and feels so right."

"This is all you," I say. "You asked the questions, pushed the buttons, forced me to look at things that I would never have looked at on my own, or with anyone else I've ever written with."

She drops her gaze, and when she looks back up at me, I can see exactly what my words have meant to her. "That makes me feel so good, Klein, but this is your song. No one else could sing this but you. It's your story."

"I really don't know how to thank you."

"There's no need," she says, "and you know, I don't want writing credit for this because this one isn't mine."

"Oh, it is," I say, "and you will definitely be getting co-writer status."

"You don't have to do that," she says. "Honestly, it was such a pleasure to spend these last few hours creating something that turned out so right."

"Want to play it through one more time?" I ask.

"Sure," she says.

"Just one thing, though."

"What's that?"

"You have to sing it with me."

"Oh no," she says. "You sing."

"Nope. That's my final request before we send this out into the world."

"Fine," she concedes, reluctant.

"Seriously, come on over here. Sit by me."

She gets up from her chair, reluctantly walks over to sit on the corner of the bed. "I'll whisper sing, how about that?" she says.

I laugh. "Real singing."

She places the laptop on the coffee table in front of us, positioning the screen so that we can both see the lyrics I typed up in their final version.

"Okay," I say, and strum the intro. I start, and it takes Dillon a line or two to sing the words where I can actually hear them. But before we reach the end of the first verse, I glance over at her. Her eyes are closed, and she's feeling the words as well as singing them. I realize how much I've loved this entire process with her, starting with the title and a few words, and then creating this song we're now singing. How I haven't felt this kind of energy for my music in a very long time.

When we reach the last word of the outro, I put my guitar across the bed and say, "Wow. That was amazing."

"Yeah, it was," Dillon says. "Who needs drugs or alcohol? Oh, I'm sorry. I didn't mean—"

"No need to apologize. I agree. This is way better than anything alcohol ever did for me."

"I'll be happy if you never play that anywhere outside of this room. It's just really nice to have made it with you."

"I don't think I can keep this one locked up."

She looks pleased by this.

"I think I'm ready for bed. Are you tired?"

"I should be," she says, "but I'm still a little wired from the coffee and the writing. Maybe I'll take a hot bath. That usually puts me right to sleep. Would you like to brush your teeth or do whatever in the bathroom before I use the bathtub?"

"Brush my teeth, and I'll be done," I say.

I go in the bathroom and close the door, reaching for my shave case and pulling out my toothbrush.

I stare at it for a moment, my thoughts hanging on Dillon, and how different she is from Riley. I glance in the mirror and see the truth in my eyes. I had known from the beginning what kind of person Riley was—that she thrived on fame and money and status. And that had never been me. Still wasn't, and I wonder what had made me think I wanted that in the woman in my life, and why it had taken me so long to figure out that I didn't.

I think about Dillon again, picture the absolute joy on her face when we unraveled another line of the song and discovered that it worked. It's been a very long time since I've enjoyed doing anything with anyone as much as I enjoyed writing that song with Dillon. And I realize, tossing my toothbrush back into the case, that I don't want to go to bed yet. I don't want this night to end.

Klein

"So was I once myself a swinger of birches.
And so I dream of going back to be."
—**Robert Frost**, *Birches*

WE END UP at the hotel's indoor swimming pool.

It's located in the spa, which is open for guests twenty-four hours around the clock. I'm already in the pool waiting for Dillon. She's in the women's dressing area, changing.

I swim a couple of laps from one end of the pool to the other, feeling completely wide awake now. Dillon stands at the top of the stairs by the entrance to the pool, dressed in one of the spa's oversized white robes. She walks down the stairs to stop beside me, looking down with a shy smile.

"You're lucky I put a bathing suit in my suitcase."

"I am lucky," I say, looking up at her with a smile.

She rolls her eyes and says, "I didn't mean it like that. I just meant I considered not bringing one, but then I always take a bathing suit on any kind of trip just in case there's time to jump in a pool somewhere."

"So, jump in," I say, my tone teasing now.

Her eyes widen a bit, and then she says, "Stop."

"Stop what?"

"You know."

"What?"

"Flirting," she says.

"Oh, is that what I'm doing?"

"Yes, I believe it is."

"So hop in, and I'll stop."

"I'm not sure I believe you, but okay."

She walks over to one of the poolside lounge chairs, slips off the spa slippers, and then unties her robe. I make myself look away. One, because I know she wants me to. Two, because I'm afraid I'm getting myself in trouble here. Even so, I can't stop myself from looking up when she walks down the stairs.

She deliberately avoids my gaze, dropping quickly into the water and swimming for the far end of the pool. She does two laps back and forth before stopping in the middle, arms wrapped around herself, breathing hard.

"Impressive," I say. "You swim for exercise?"

"Yeah," she says. "I try to do five days a week. My knees stopped liking running, so I had to find something that would still get my heart rate up, but not be so hard on the joints. I jog here and there, but mostly when it's somewhere I want to see."

"You have a strong stroke."

"I was a terrible swimmer at first. I had to work at it to get remotely respectable. I even took some lessons at one of the clubs in Nashville, me, and all the other six-year-olds there."

I laugh. "Hey, sometimes you got to ditch the pride to get where you need to be."

"That is very true," she says. "What do you do for fitness?"

"I like to run, and I hit the gym a few times a week. Don't want to be the only band member who can't lug a piece of heavy equipment on stage."

She looks at me, a little surprised. "You still do that?"

I shrug. "I like to be a part of the whole picture, and I did those things from the very beginning. I don't see any reason to change that up."

"Some people would see plenty of reason."

"I'm not those people."

"No, you certainly are not," she agrees.

"I didn't tell you that for admiration or anything like that. It's just that I see myself as a regular guy, and regular guys don't stand around waiting for other people to do things for them."

"That's not what Josh would say," she says, the words

coming out so fast that I wonder if she would like to take them back.

"I'm sure he's done his version of hard work," I say. "He wouldn't be where he is if that weren't true."

"Yeah."

"What happened between you two?" I ask before I can give myself time to reconsider. "I mean I know he had an affair, but what went wrong before that?"

She folds her arms across her chest and looks off at the other end of the pool. Several long seconds pass before she answers, and when she does, her voice is so low that I wonder if I have imagined her answer.

"These," she says, waving four fingers across the center of her chest. "These went wrong. They're not real. They look it in this bathing suit, though, don't they?"

I have no idea what to say, so I just keep my face blank and wait for her to go on.

"I had breast cancer about three years ago, and these are the outcome of the surgery I decided to have when all was said and done. They weren't enough for Josh. I think it was the whole not-really-real thing that got him. In the hospital after my mastectomy, the nurses were changing my bandages. Josh caught a glimpse between the crack in the curtain. I remember the look on his face, and how utterly horrified he was. And every time I think about how I looked after that surgery, that's what I remember because his expression was an exact, honest, description of what had been done to me. Of who I had become."

I hear the break in her voice and slosh through the water to stand in front of her. I feel as if my own chest has cracked open. I reach out a thumb to wipe the tears leaking from her eyes. I wrap my arms around her and pull her to me, holding on tight, as if I can absorb the pain of hurt in her voice. Pain that is still so clearly there. I feel the sobs start, her shoulders shaking under their weight.

"Hey," I say, pulling back to look down at her and brushing my hand across her cheek. "It's okay. I'm sorry I opened that up. I didn't know."

"Of course, you didn't. I don't know why I told you. You certainly didn't need to hear all of that. I mean, I'm fine."

"Are you?" I ask, and I realize how very much I need to hear that this is true, that she is fine. I take her hand and lead her to the side of the pool, lift her up, and set her on the edge. I hoist myself up to sit next to her. "I never heard anything about you being sick."

"I didn't want anyone to know," she says. "To be honest, after Josh's reaction, I was kind of terrified to tell anyone because I didn't want them to see me as that songwriter with cancer. I just wanted to keep being me. Dillon Blake, the girl I'd always been."

My heart hurts with sympathy. "How long were you sick?"

She shrugs. "All said and done almost two years. Everything is good now as far as I know. Last scan said so, anyway."

I hear her attempt at nonchalance, but there's nothing light about this. "I can't even imagine how painful what you went through must have been. And that's what should have mattered. Your pain. Your suffering. Not how you looked."

Tears stream down her face, and I don't even bother to wipe them away. I just pull her up against me and wrap my arms tight around her, so tight that I might somehow keep the pain she still feels about that time in her life from breaking her in half.

I hold her for a long time while she cries quietly. I don't know how long we sit that way before she says in a soft voice, "I really should not have unloaded all of this on you."

"I wish I had known. Even as a friend, Dillon, I would have liked to have been there for you."

She pulls back, looking at me, and this time, she's the one who puts a hand to my face and leans up to kiss me, softly, and with gratitude, at first. And then with increasing passion, pressing her body against mine. There is no hiding the fact that I want her.

I brush my hand across her flat stomach and then, upwards to the curve of her breast. She gasps a little, and I say, "Does that hurt?"

"No," she says. "No. It doesn't hurt. It's just—I haven't been touched since—"

And it is then that I would really like to choke the life from Josh Cummings. "Can I tell you something?"

"Yes," she says.

"I never thought Josh deserved you."

"You're just saying that to be nice."

"No, I am not," I say. "You know that night at the Bluebird when you came up to me about the signing, and then we talked in the parking lot?"

"I remember."

"I knew you were married, and yet, I still wanted to ask you to come home with me that night. And I would have if I'd thought you would say yes. I would have tossed you in my truck and taken you back to my place and not let you out for a very long time."

She laughs. Surprised, and a little disbelieving. "No, you would not have."

"Oh yes, I would have," I say. "I could barely think about what you were saying about signing with Top Dog because I was too busy looking at your face and noticing how great you looked in that pair of jeans. And yeah, the sweater you had on that night, it was hard not to notice what was beneath that as well." I drop my gaze to her swim top. "I'm looking at you now and thinking exactly what I thought that night."

I raise my gaze to her face then, note the flush stealing

up her cheeks. I keep my gaze on hers, not closing my eyes until just before I sink my mouth onto hers. Dillon releases an audible sigh, slipping her arms around my neck and pressing her breasts to my chest.

I slip back into the pool and anchor one hand on each side of her waist, sliding her forward into the water so that I'm standing between her legs. Luckily, there's no one else around. It's the middle of the night. I am aware that this could get out of hand fast. But I don't want to stop kissing her, and I don't.

We go on for several minutes until Dillon finally drops her head back, and says, "We have to stop. We'll get arrested for indecent exposure."

"I'm not exposing anything. Are you exposing anything?" I say, smiling.

"Well, no, but I could see things moving in that direction."

I don't bother to hide my disappointment. "Okay. You're right. It's almost morning, but why don't we head to the room and get a couple of hours of sleep before we figure out what we're going to do with a full day in Paris?"

She leans up and kisses me once more, and then, with clear reluctance, turns and climbs the steps out of the pool.

Josh

"There was a long hard time when I kept far from me the remembrance of what I had thrown away when I was quite ignorant of its worth."
—**Charles Dickens,** *Great Expectations*

IT'S TEN IN the morning in Paris, nowhere near daybreak in Nashville, but I haven't slept all night anyway, so I might as well make the call. Since Riley sent me that damn photo from that gossip rag magazine yesterday afternoon, I haven't been able to think of anything else. I question her motivation, but it's probably not that difficult to figure out. Klein broke up with her, and she's jealous that he's hanging out with Dillon and hoping I'll have some influence over ending that.

Her attempt to get me to intervene should not have mattered. Dillon and I are getting a divorce, so why would I care what she's doing with Klein aside from the obvious business interests, of course? The question is, then, why have I not been able to stop thinking about it? And what is this hammer of jealousy that keeps pounding me in the heart? I really thought I didn't care what Dillon does anymore or who she's with. I realize that I have no right to question anything she does. I know I've hurt her terribly. Maybe I need to be forgiven, to hear from her that she doesn't see me as the monster she has every right to see me as.

I pour myself another cup of coffee from the pot I'd made over an hour ago. It's not as good as it was fresh, but I take a fortifying sip and pick up my phone, calling Dillon's number. By the fourth ring, I'm pretty sure she's not going to answer. When I hear her voice, I'm silent for a long moment, not sure what to say.

"Josh," she says, her voice groggy.

"Are you still asleep?" I say, and then taking the edge from the question, "Isn't it like ten o'clock there?"

"Yeah," she says, and I can hear her trying to wake up. "Late night."

"Ah," I say. "What kept you up so late?"

She sighs and says, "Josh, what do you want?"

"I don't know. I was hoping we could talk."

"About what?"

"About us."

"There is no us," she says. "Remember?"

"Yeah, I know. I just—"

"What?" she says. "You just what?"

171

"I guess I've been thinking that it seems a shame to throw away what we had."

"Oh, and what has you thinking this, Josh?"

"I don't know. You being gone. I saw that picture of you with Klein in a magazine."

She makes a sound of disbelief. "So you're telling me now that you're jealous after I spent how long throwing myself at you to no avail as your wife? You didn't want me, Josh. Why would you want me now? Because someone else is trying to play with your toy?"

"Don't be crude," I say.

"I'm not being crude. You're like a little boy, Josh. Even when you're tired of your toy, you don't want anyone else to have it."

"That's not how I see it," I say.

"It's how it is," she fires back. "Is it so shocking to you that someone else might want me?"

"No," I say quietly. "It's not shocking to me at all."

She's silent then for a stretch of moments, and I can feel her grappling for words. "Is this really just an attempt on your part to get me to not go into competition against you?"

"No," I say. "It's not. People deserve second chances, Dillon. That's all I'm asking for."

"So what happened to the fact that you were bringing your lover to Paris less than forty-eight hours ago?"

I hesitate, several long beats of silence hanging between

172

our phones. "I guess I started trying to picture myself there with her, and I couldn't. I could only see myself there with you." He expects a sharp comeback from Dillon, but he doesn't get one.

Her voice is soft when she says, "How am I supposed to believe that, Josh?"

"I don't know. You have every right not to," I say, "but it's the truth nonetheless."

"You can't just. . .you've hurt me, Josh. Surely you know that."

"I do, and I can't even begin to tell you how sorry I am. I was horrible to you. When you were sick, I should've been there for you, and I couldn't get past my own needs long enough to think about yours."

"That's true," she says.

"I am ashamed of myself, Dillon, really. You have no idea. It keeps me awake at night."

"That's not going to change anything, though, is it?" she asks. "I don't want to spend the rest of my life hating you for the bad times in our marriage, but I admit I've wondered whether or not you ever really loved me, Josh, because when you love someone, you do want to take away their pain in any way you can."

"I know," I say. "You're right. I wish I could go back and do things over again. Honestly, Dillon, it would be so different. I promise you it would. When you get back, can we talk? It doesn't have to be anything more than that. Just

173

let me know when you can come, and I'll meet you at the house.'"

"I don't want to meet you at the house."

"Then, somewhere neutral. You name the place."

"I'll think about it, Josh, but I have to go now."

"Okay," I say. "Please call me, okay?"

She hangs up without answering.

I put my phone on the kitchen counter, place both palms against the molding, and drop my head forward, letting out a long breath. I want things to be the way they used to be, before I let Dillon down so badly and before my stupidity with Leanne. Dillon and I had a good life together. It wasn't perfect, but it was good. And if she'll give me a chance, I will make her remember that as well.

Dillon

"No matter what the work you are doing, be always ready
to drop it. And plan it, so as to be able to leave it."
—**Leo Tolstoy,** *The Journal of Leo Tolstoy*

I WALK BACK into the bedroom, sure that I look as
confused as I feel.

"Is everything all right?" Klein asks. He's sitting on the
corner of the bed, pulling on a pair of running shoes. His
hair is wet from the shower.

The simple act of setting eyes on him sends a zing
through my center. "Yeah, I guess so. That was Josh."

"Ah," Klein says. "Anything in particular that he called
about?"

"He saw that picture of us, and I don't know what he
started thinking. He asked to see me when I get back to
Nashville."

Klein keeps his gaze on the shoestrings he's tying and

then looks up at me, his response measured. "Do you want to see him?"

"I don't know," I say, lifting my shoulders in a half shrug. "No, not really. I'm angry at him and can't imagine what else there is for us to say to each other. But he did apologize, and he sounds like he really meant it. A part of me thinks I should hear him out."

"Would you consider going back to him?" Klein asks, his voice neutral.

"No," I say, shaking my head. "All the things that were broken between us aren't fixable."

"But you loved him at one time."

"Yes, I did, or at least I thought I did. I thought he loved me, but that didn't pan out when times got tough. I just know now that I don't want to be with anyone who can't be there for me through all of it."

"You're right to want that." Klein looks as if he would like to say more, but he doesn't. He stands and changes the subject. "So, where are we headed today?"

"I've always wanted to see Versailles," I say.

"Then Versailles it is."

~

IT'S MIDAFTERNOON by the time we finish touring the grounds. I could have stayed so much longer, fascinated by the history, the wealth that must have been needed to build such a palace. It's actually unimaginable that so much could have been put into a home for the king.

We're leaving the grounds when I wonder out loud, "Don't you think it's amazing that the people of that time would be okay with so much of the country's wealth going into the king's residence. Surely there was poverty that could have been lessened with some of those resources."

"Yeah. I've wondered about that myself," Klein says. "I guess people take pride in their country and want their heads of state to be an example to the world."

"I think if I were king, I wouldn't feel too great about living in a place like this when there were people in my country who didn't have a roof over their heads. I guess it's like most things human though. We convince ourselves that we deserve certain things even when we really don't."

We take an Uber back to the hotel. It's almost two o'clock by the time we get to the room. We consider room service for lunch because we're both tired from our late night. But then I think of all the wonderful places to eat on the streets surrounding us. "Why don't we walk and see what we find?" I suggest.

"Sounds good to me," Klein says. We leave the hotel, decide to turn left in the square. It's been a beautiful day, and the sun is still bright above us, the sky a vivid, cloudless blue. We walk in silence for the first few minutes. I'm content to take in our surroundings, shops, small local groceries, cafés where people sit outside.

A few blocks from the hotel, we pass a place to eat that looks particularly inviting. "What about this one?"

"Sure," Klein says.

We wait at the entrance podium until a young woman comes and leads us to a table under the outside awning. We're seated with our menus when I look at Klein and say, "Is everything all right? You've been kind of quiet."

"I'm good," he says. I start to let it go, but then he looks back at me and says, "I guess that's not really true."

"What, then?"

"The call from Josh. It just reminded me that we have reality to return to, and none of this, what we've been doing here, is reality."

The statement surprises me. I guess it hadn't occurred to me that he cared one way or the other. "I wish we could stay."

"Me, too."

"We're both scheduled to leave tomorrow," I say.

"We are," he agrees. "You know, I've been working on the new album I'm contracted for, and honestly, before this trip, nothing was coming to me. I had kind of reached the point where I thought I would just need to tell my label that I've got nothing and let them do with that whatever they wanted to. But after we wrote that song last night, I don't know, it's like maybe a valve has been opened up again, and I really have the desire to write. But I'd like to do it with you, Dillon."

"Really? In Nashville?"

"Actually, I was wondering what you would think of taking some time to drive around the countryside, stay wherever we feel like staying, and write while we're still here."

"That would be absolutely incredible," I say. "I would love to do that."

He smiles then, and I realize it's his first genuine smile of the day, or since this morning, at least. "No one's expecting you back?"

"No one who can't wait," he says. "And you?"

"No, not really," I say, thinking of Josh, and then blinking the thought away as quickly as it has appeared.

And, as if he has read my mind, Klein says, "Josh?"

"I don't feel like I owe Josh anything. But, if he wants to have a face-to-face conversation with me, that can certainly wait."

"Good," Klein says, smiling again. "So, where should we go?"

~

WE ORDER LUNCH from the mouthwatering menu, and while we're waiting on our food, we start googling places to visit outside Paris. We find a few small towns that sound absolutely wonderful, and then Klein says,

"You know, we're not confined to France. We can go wherever we want. Train, car."

I laugh a little. "Hold on, now. If you're not careful, I might not ever let you get back to Nashville."

"I'm starting to think I wouldn't have a problem with that."

A wave of warmth cascades through my midsection, and I don't think I'm crazy to think that he's flirting with me. It very much feels like flirting, and I cannot deny that it feels amazing. "Careful what you wish for," I say.

"Oh, I am very, very careful," Klein says. And before I can ask him to elaborate on that, the waitress has returned with our food. We're both distracted by how wonderful it looks and how hungry we are. I've ordered an enormous mixed veggie salad, Klein, an omelet with herbs, and we both dig in as if we haven't eaten in a week.

Once we've satisfied a bit of our hunger, Klein looks at me and says, "I think I could easily gain fifty pounds here."

"Me, too," I say, "but it would look far better on you than me."

"Highly debatable," he says.

When we're finished, we both decline dessert but opt for a coffee. As we're sipping, I pick up my phone and try another search for great places to visit near Paris. There are so many that sound amazing that it's almost overwhelming. I spot a link called Horse Vacations, and out of curiosity, click on it.

"Do you ride?" I ask Klein, without looking up from the screen.

"Anything in particular?" he asks, and I can feel his smile.

I look up and meet his gaze with a pointed, "Horses, of course."

"I might have been on one or two at a county fair," he says.

"Oh my gosh, look at this," I say, turning the screen to face him. "It's a château in the Bordeaux region. You can stay there, plus they have horseback riding excursions. For all levels of riders."

I scroll through the photos, and he nods once and says, "Let's go there."

"Really?" I say. "It can't be that easy."

"It looks like a great place, and why not? We'll rent a car and drive. How far is it?"

"It looks like maybe six hours," I say. "That might be a little far."

"Nope," he says.

I lean back and study him for a moment. "You know, you're amazingly easy."

"I hope you mean that in the nicest way possible," he says.

"Josh and I could never agree on places to go or

181

restaurants to try. I don't know," I say, shaking my head and shrugging a little bit. "It was like it was always a battle for some reason."

"Control?" Klein says.

"I guess. I don't know. It always seemed like it should be way easier than it was."

"It should be," Klein says.

"Are you just this easygoing?" I ask.

"Not when it comes to certain things," he says. "Like when it comes to picking songs to release, I'm not very easy to deal with. I'm a perfectionist, I guess, and I don't want to send anything out to my audience that they wouldn't think was my absolute best effort in a song."

"Well, no one could fault you for that. That's actually a good thing. How about in relationships?"

"I don't know that I'm the one to ask about that," he says. "But no, I'm definitely not the easiest person to be around sometimes."

"I haven't seen that," I say.

"Well, you haven't been in a car with me for six hours, either," he says.

I laugh. "True. Tomorrow?"

"Tomorrow," he says, and smiles.

Dillon

"Catherine had never wanted comfort more, and [Henry]
looked as if he was aware of it."
—Jane Austen, *Northanger Abbey*

WE SPEND THE rest of the afternoon planning for our
departure in the morning. I take care of reserving the car.
Klein handles contacting the château, and, thankfully, they
do have two rooms available. I do notice that he's asked for
two, and, of course, he would. He's a gentleman.

But some part of me admittedly wants this uninterrupted
time I've had with him since we've been sharing a room to
continue. I have no right to expect it. And our sharing a
room had been necessary. Now that reality is setting back
in, it is time to admit that basically, we are two friends
who've ended up in an unexpected situation together. And
now that we've agreed to write some songs, we're going
to take a bit of time to do that. Nothing more, Dillon, I tell
myself.

183

By the time we finish making all the arrangements, it's after eight o'clock, and we're both not very hungry because we'd had a late lunch. We decide to order a pizza and share it. We're sitting on the bed with the pizza between us, each of us taking a slice, when Klein says, "I'm really psyched about this. I can't remember the last time I did anything spontaneous. Mostly by necessity, but most of my life seems to be planned down to every minute of every hour."

I sense that he's serious, so I decide not to make light of this. "I guess that's one of the pitfalls of being famous," I say. "You have so many people wanting something from you, and there's only so much of you to go around."

"True, but, you know," he says, "I feel like I owe people who helped me along the way. And I do want to pay back as much of that as I can, but—"

"People get used to asking, don't they?"

"It's not that I don't understand. I remember what it feels like to be hungry for success, to be looking for any notch in the ladder that might help me climb a little faster. Admittedly, the more successful I've become, the harder it is for people to reach me. But, I don't know, I guess when someone does ask for help, I feel obligated because of my own good fortune to do what I can. To those whom much is given, much is expected?"

"I feel the same," I say. "But, of course, my success is not in the same stratosphere as yours."

"What you've accomplished is amazing. I certainly haven't been named songwriter of the year."

"Thanks," I say. "It's not. . .I don't mean to demean what I've done. It's just, it is all relative, you know. And you do so much for others, Klein. I do try to find things that I think might be a little unique to me as far as how I can help others. There's a program for creative kids who might not have the financial means to develop those talents outside of regular school. I do some work with them a couple of afternoons a week, and it's been incredibly rewarding. You wouldn't believe how crazy talented some of these kids are. There's this one little boy named Raymond who, honestly, could be the next van Gogh. He paints, and he just has this unique fingerprint for his art that, when you see something he's done, you automatically know it's his, and you recognize the look. It's really fascinating, and I have so enjoyed encouraging him and looking for ways to bring out his talent even more."

"That is wonderful," Klein says. "I've often thought about how many kids might have even the same set of talents that I have, if I have any," he modestly corrects himself, "and just never get the chance to be heard or seen. It's such a waste."

"It is. I really believe we all have some talent that is unique to us as individuals, and it might get beaten down by so many different things. Poverty, someone putting us down at some point early on and making us doubt our

185

abilities. I was lucky to have a mother who really was the opposite of that. She wanted me to be the next Dolly Parton." I laugh a little and shake my head. "Minus the obvious attributes, of course."

Klein smiles. "Tell me about her."

"My mom?"

"Yeah."

"She was amazing, really. She didn't grow up with much, and we didn't have a lot materially when I was little. She worked full-time at a sewing factory in our town. She made all my clothes, and we would go to Leggett's on Saturday mornings to pick out a new pattern and fabric for something she would make me the following week. It was like I had my own Vogue catalog and seamstress willing to create whatever I had a fancy for that Saturday, whether it was a pair of shorts with daisies around the hem, or a sundress made from purple velvet. She was willing to make it for me.

"I actually think I get my creativity from my mama. She never had the opportunity to use hers beyond the things that she did for me, and the way she decorated our house. But she had an amazing talent for those things. And if she'd had opportunities when she was in school, and then the chance to go on to college, I know she would have been able to use her creativity in other ways as well."

"Is that why you've chosen the volunteering that you do?"

"It is," I say. "I mean, selfishly, I kind of had my mom all to myself, and she loved doing those things for me so much. But sometimes I wish she could have been recognized by others as well for her contributions to the world."

"Is your mom still—"

"No," I say. "She died five years ago. Cancer."

"I'm sorry," Klein says.

"There isn't a day that goes by that I don't miss her with this hole inside me that I know will never be filled. She used to use country music songs to give me lessons in life. She said country music songwriters were better than therapists, that they already had all the problems defined and the answers figured out. So, if I would just keep listening to country music, I would never need a therapist."

Klein laughs softly. "I would love to have met her."

"I would have loved for her to know you." I press my lips together and look away, wondering if I have revealed too much in the seriousness with which I have voiced this.

"I've felt that same guilt," Klein says. "Kind of like survivor guilt, I guess. I wonder why I'm the generation who didn't succumb to drugs, why I was able to untangle myself from the snare of addiction, and why both of my parents couldn't do that. It's easy to declare a person completely bad, and I went through a good number of years where I was convinced there wouldn't have been anything good to find in either my mom or dad.

"But I think I know now that we're all made up of good and bad, and I wonder what would have happened to them if they had had the opportunity to be exposed to a different life, a chance to clean up their act, and the kind of rehab facility I went to. I know they wouldn't have had that chance because there wasn't money for that kind of thing. But somehow, I don't know, it doesn't really seem fair, does it? That I should get a second chance for my bad choices, but they didn't."

"No," I say. "It doesn't seem fair, and that's the sort of thing about life that I have no explanation for."

"Did your mom get sick before you—" He breaks off there as if he's rethinking the question.

But I understand what he's asking, and say, "No, she died before I got sick. I don't know. I've wondered sometimes if the stress of losing her might have been what caused whatever was brewing inside of me to get an advantage."

"How long was she sick?" he asks. "Not very long, or at least not that we knew. She died within three months of the cancer being discovered."

"So it was a shock to you," he says with audible sympathy.

"Very much so. She was in the hospital because she'd had a reaction to one of the chemo drugs they were giving her, and I had spent the afternoon with her. But Josh and I had something we were supposed to go to that night, and

I debated not going. My mom insisted because she felt so much better, and they were planning to send her home the next morning. So, I went, and she died at eleven that night while we were at a party." Tears shred my voice, and I drop my head, trying to blink them away, but there's no stopping them now. They've reached the surface, and sobs shake my shoulders.

Klein reaches for me, pulls me into the curve of his arm, and hugs me hard. I try to stop crying, but something about being held this way, comforted this way, makes me realize I never really got that from anyone after Mama died. Josh tried, but he never understood just how much I loved my mother. I think I tried to hide some of my grief from him. I didn't want to feel ridiculed or questioned about my sadness. I just wanted it to be.

"Shh," Klein says, kissing my forehead. "It's okay. I'm here."

I don't know how long we sit there on the bed, me wrapped in his arms, sobbing quietly against his chest. But when my renewed grief finally eases, I realize how much I needed that, and say in a low voice, "I don't think I even knew how much of that was still knotted up inside me. I'm sorry."

"Don't be sorry," Klein says. "Clearly, she loved you so much, and she deserves to be missed like this."

"I do miss her," I say, biting my lower lip, still resting my cheek against his chest. "Sometimes I would give anything just to be able to pick up the phone and call her to hear her say, 'Hey, sweetie, how are you?' Until I lost her, I never understood how rare the kind of love she had for me is. And I didn't have any brothers or sisters. It's just a fact that once we lose our parents and grandparents, no one in our lives will ever love us like that again."

Klein pushes me back a little, so he can look down at me. "You do deserve to be loved like that, Dillon. And the right husband would love you like that. It's supposed to be unconditional. Isn't that what marriage vows are supposed to be about?"

"Yeah," I say, "they are supposed to be that. But mine didn't end up being like that."

"I don't think that's your fault," he says softly.

"I wasn't the perfect wife by any stretch, Klein. I'm not trying to say that I was."

"I know," he says. "I wish I'd had a chance to meet your mother."

"I wish you had, too," I say with a teary smile. "Oh my gosh. She would have been so in love with you." I realize then exactly how much I've said and break off there.

"That could only be the highest compliment, given the woman you've described."

I sit up, rub at a spot on his T-shirt. "Somehow, I managed to get pizza sauce on you."

He smiles. "No biggie."

I sit up, throw my legs over the side of the bed, my

back to him now. "Thank you, Klein, for listening. I really didn't mean to open all of that up, but I do appreciate your kindness."

"You don't need to thank me, Dillon. That's what friends are for, a shoulder to lean on when you need it."

I nod, still not facing him. Friends, that is what we are, and he truly is an amazing one. But I need to remember that this isn't more than that, and that it's not ever going to be more.

Klein

"The world is a book and those who do not travel read
only one page."
—St. Augustine

WE BOTH FALL asleep on the bed watching a movie.
I wake up sometime in the middle of the night to find
Dillon curled up against me, and it takes a few moments
for me to remember where I am and who it is I'm in
bed with. I start to move but then decide against it, not
wanting to wake her. She makes a small sound of protest
and curls closer. I stare at the ceiling and count to thirty.
I force myself to recite lyrics, anything to keep my mind
from wandering to the obvious fact that there's a beautiful
woman wrapped around me, and I can't do a thing about
it.

I probably count a couple of thousand sheep by the time
I actually fall asleep again. The next time I wake up, it's

morning, and the sunlight is streaming in through a crack in the curtains. I feel a jolt on the other side of the bed, turn my head to see Dillon looking at me with wide eyes. "I'm sorry. I meant to sleep on the couch," she says.

"It's not a problem," I say. "We were both out like a light. That doesn't say a lot for the movie, though."

"No, it doesn't," she says. "Would you like some coffee if I order some?"

"I would love some." I walk to the bathroom and close the door, turning on the shower and stepping under the cold spray. When I come back out, a silver tray sits on the corner of the bed. Dillon is sipping from a cup of coffee.

"Sorry, I couldn't wait," she says. "It smelled too good."

"It does smell good." I pour myself a cup and say, "What time was the rental car company dropping off the car?"

"Nine," she says. "It should be out front waiting for us."

"That gives us about forty-five minutes to get packed up and checked out."

"I'm going to grab a quick shower," Dillon says, and disappears into the bathroom with her coffee.

Once she's no longer in the room, I drop down on to the bed, take another fortifying sip of coffee, and ask myself if the two of us spending more time together is really a good idea. My life is pretty much a mess. Dillon's not even divorced yet. And I'm playing with fire. I do know that much. I think about waking up in the middle of the night and realizing she was in bed beside me, and one thing I know for sure is we can't be sharing a bed. I don't have that much faith in my willpower.

Would it be wiser to tell Dillon we should just get together for some writing sessions in Nashville? I am pretty sure that would be the smart thing to do. But it isn't what I *want to* do.

~

A BELLMAN COLLECTS our luggage from the room, and we meet him at the entrance to the hotel. I've already checked out by calling the front desk and settling the bill. A young man greets us at the rental car, handing me the keys and wishing us a pleasant journey.

The make and model aren't one I recognize, so I'm assuming it's a European manufacturer. I look at Dillon and dangle the keys. "Would you like to drive?"

"I think I will leave that up to you," she says.

"I'm not making any promises. I've driven in LA, but I'm not sure how that will compare to this."

"We'll see," she says, smiling and sliding into the passenger seat.

I get in, my knees hitting the dashboard under the steering wheel. "Ouch." I move the seat back as far as it will go.

"I'm not sure this car is going to be big enough," Dillon says.

"We'll make do."

"We could remove the driver's seat, and you could sit in

the back," she says, giggling. It's the first time I've heard her laugh like that, and I realize with a jolt how much I enjoy being the one to cause it.

"Reverse chauffeuring, or something like that." She giggles again, and I make an attempt to stab the key in the ignition, finally finding it and starting the car. It makes a rattling sound that causes us both to look at each other with a question mark on our faces.

"Ah, do you think they gave us a good car?" Dillon asks.

"Remains to be seen," I say. "We could take it back or just go with it. A rattling muffler outside the Ritz Paris is a bit of a contraindication, but we'll see where we get."

"Okay," Dillon says, not hiding the skepticism in her voice.

The car is a manual shift, and it's been a long time since I drove anything other than an automatic. I let the clutch out, and we lurch forward. I hit the brake. The tires squeal. Dillon is laughing full force now, and I glance out the window to see a frowning hotel employee clearly ready for us to get this jalopy out of the square. I give another try, and we're off, fairly smoothly this time. I turn the car onto the street, stopping at a red light.

"Okay, now. No more making fun of my driving. Have you got the GPS on?"

"Yes," Dillon says, still trying not to laugh. She props her phone on the ledge above the car's radio and points at the map. "We're here, and we're going there."

"Let's hope we make it," I say.

"You sure we shouldn't change out cars?"

"Too late now," I say. "We're off."

The Paris traffic is definitely different from Nashville, but it's not LA. I manage to get us to the outskirts of the city without incidence. I give Dillon a side glance. "Sure you don't want to drive?"

"Oh, no, you're doing excellent," she says. "And besides, I don't know how to drive a straight. That would be disastrous. When did you learn how to drive a straight?"

"Somewhere along the way. One of my buddies in high school had an old farm use truck he used to take out in his granddaddy's hayfield and cut up on. He taught me how to drive it one Saturday night when he'd had a few too many. He started me out on a hill, I guess because he thought it would add a little humor to the situation and that if I could conquer that, I'd be good to go."

Dillon smiles. "Were you?"

"Pretty much, after we rolled backward a dozen or so times."

Dillon smiles, and I can tell she is picturing my learning curve. "So tell me about this place we're going to," I say.

"Okay," she says, picking up her phone and tapping out of the map screen. "It's a château that was built in the sixteenth century. Obviously renovated since then. They have a vineyard and make their own label of wine. They have an orchard and use the peaches and pears they grow in the foods made in the restaurant. They have a barn of forty horses that do various disciplines, including jumping. That one I'm sure you will want to do," she says, cocking me a smile.

"Of course, absolutely," I say.

"They have ponies for children. They have horses for trail riding and some dressage."

"Dressage. What exactly is that?"

"That is a discipline in which the horse is taught certain movements at the most basic level and advances up the chain of difficulty. It's beautiful to watch, sort of like a horse dancing."

"Sounds beautiful," I say. "You'll be doing that, right?"

She shakes her head and smiles. "No, I'll be doing whatever the most basic riding form they have available is. Walk, trot."

"Oh, good. Then possibly, I'll be able to keep up with you."

"No doubt," she says.

"What else do they have?" I ask.

"There's a spa with a sauna and a cold therapy room. You can get massages, facials, sports pedicures. That one I'll be signing you up for," she says.

"Ha. Men don't get pedicures."

"Well, they should. It's just another form of self-care," she says.

"And I've never had one," I say.

"I'll be happy to get one with you," she suggests. "It's actually incredibly relaxing. The techs massage your feet and buff them up so they look all neat and clean."

I laugh. "Okay, I'm wondering if there's some implication there."

"No," she says. "But why wouldn't men want to keep their feet neat? That's one of those stigmas that somehow got created because someone thought it was sissy to have your feet pampered."

"I'll agree with that. In my town, there weren't too many men going to Lou Ann's Nails to get their feet pampered."

She laughs now outright. "You could start a trend. The first time you showed up at Lou Ann's, everybody would be on their cell phone posting on Facebook how they saw you getting a pedicure, and then before you know it, half the men in your hometown will be calling for appointments."

Now it's my turn to laugh. "Oh, you think that's how it would go, huh?"

"I'm sure of it. You know sometimes, men just need to see a guy they admire doing something to think it's okay for them to do it, too."

"So this is my new mission in life. Saving men from their feet."

She's laughing so hard now she can't speak. "I think it's an admirable undertaking," she finally manages.

"Forget world peace, curing hunger, things like that." We're both laughing now, and once I have myself under control again, I say, "It's amazingly easy to be around you, Dillon." I feel her looking at me, glance her way to see her eyes are still warm with laughter.

"It's pretty easy to be around you too," she says.

"I can't really say that of many of the people I've been close to in my life," I say.

"What do you mean?" she asks.

I shrug, passing a car and then cutting back into the right lane. "I don't know. It seems like most of the people I've had relationships with tend to be difficult, controlling, I guess."

"Do you think that's been deliberate on your part?"

"I don't know," I say. "Maybe."

"Why?" she asks.

"That would be the million-dollar question. The obvious choice would be to choose to be around people who make life lighter, easier, more fun."

"Well, I definitely didn't choose someone like that," Dillon says. "Do you think we pick someone opposite from ourselves?"

"Maybe, although, unless we don't like ourselves, I guess that doesn't make a lot of sense."

"Or maybe we think we need someone different from us to complete the picture."

"Yeah, or maybe we think somewhere down deep that

we don't really deserve to be happy, so we pick someone who will make sure we're not."

Dillon looks off to the side for long enough that I wonder if I've said too much. "It would be sad to think that's true," she says. "But maybe on some level, it is. Do you think you deserve to be happy, Klein?"

I answer before giving myself time to think about it. "I don't think I deserve everything I have in life."

"Why?"

"Maybe because some part of me thinks I've been lucky. That I'm not any more deserving of it than some other guy who's worked hard to develop his talent and maybe hasn't gotten anywhere with it."

"Or, do you think," she says, "it could be because of what happened in your early life? That because your parents made the choices they made, some part of you thinks that says something about you?"

I consider the question, realizing without too much thought that she's probably hit on an undeniable truth. "Maybe," I say. "I think I know why you're such a good writer."

"Well, thank you, but—"

Before she can finish, I say, "You look not only at the person but their why. You go below the surface and dig around until you've found the answer to what makes them who they are. You'd also make a good therapist if you ever decide to get out of writing."

"Ah, thank you, I think," she says.

"It's actually the highest form of compliment," I say. "You listen to what other people have to say, but you actually hear them. Not too many people can say that. Have you ever noticed how sometimes when you're talking to someone you can see in their eyes that they're not really listening, that they're actually thinking about what they're going to say when you're done?"

"Yes," she says. "So true."

"And you don't even really want to continue what you were saying because you know they're not really interested."

"Yeah," she says. "I guess we all struggle not to be that person because even though we know better and don't want to admit it, we're all actually more interested in ourselves than other people."

"True," I agree. "But to be a writer, you have to be able to hear others, and I think you do, Dillon, whether you are exactly aware of it or not."

"In all honesty, I'm not sure that I get any bonus points for that because it's probably more about my own curiosity than it is about my interest in them."

"You might be selling yourself a bit short."

"And I think you're being kind."

"Just honest," I say.

"We're all selfish on some level," Dillon says.

"The price of being human. Hard to get out of our own way, isn't it?"

"Definitely," she says, sighing. "But I don't know. After everything I went through being sick, I started seeing life differently than I had seen it before."

"How so?"

"Um, I mean, we all know we're going to die. We learn that early on in life, but somehow I'm not sure we really believe it until we're faced with our own mortality. It's like it's not real, or we think on some level that it happens to other people, but it won't really happen to us. And then one day you hit that wall where it becomes very, very clear that your body has a stop point, and things just start to look totally different." Her voice drops a note or two, serious now. She looks out the window.

"There's a reason why someone came up with that saying that youth is wasted on the young. I guess it's also wasted on the uninitiated. By that, I mean, those of us who haven't yet hit that wall, realized there really is another side, and when we do, at least for me, it was impossible to look at my life as I had looked at it before. Now, it's like I want to get as much from every day as I possibly can. I want to give back in ways that I never did before because I understand that is really the only way I can leave something of myself here. What I give to others."

She trails off there, and it's a good bit before I can bring myself to speak around the lump in my throat. "You might

202

think, Dillon, that everyone comes out the other end of what you went through feeling as you do now, but I don't think so. I think you're rare in that you took something awful that happened to you, something that would break a lot of people, and you allowed it to make you stronger. It would be very easy to let something like that break you. I'm pretty sure it would break me."

"I think you're stronger than you give yourself credit for," Dillon says.

"You're strong," I say.

"I'm stronger than I ever would have believed," she agrees, surprising me a little. "But as I go along, I realize more and more that life is full of tests, and sometimes we pass, and sometimes we fail. I'm pretty sure where Josh is concerned, I failed."

"You think you're to blame for the problems you've had."

"I feel sure I'm partially to blame. It's almost never one person who's wrong about everything. Sometimes I think I expected too much, like the fairytale version, or something. But there's no such thing as a fairytale in real life."

"No," I agree. "There isn't."

We're on the Autoroute now, a toll road, and cars are blowing past me in the left-hand lanes. I'm hugging the right lane at 130 kilometers. "Okay, given the speed of this traffic," I say, "I'm pretty sure we should have gotten a bigger car."

"It is fast, isn't it?" Dillon says. "But you're holding your own."

"Yeah, over here in the chicken lane," I say.

She laughs softly. "What do you drive back home?" she asks.

"A truck, of course."

"What kind?"

"Ford."

"So, you're a Ford man."

"Is there any other kind?"

She smiles and shakes her head. "I have a little bit of a soft spot for the Dodge, but I get the whole Ford thing. Nothing low slung for you?"

"I've toyed with the idea but never really thought it was me."

"I'm pretty sure you'd look good in a Ferrari."

"We're a long way from that," I say, patting the dashboard.

She laughs again. "Transportation and nothing more when you take ego out of the picture."

"You got that right," I say. And the car is holding up to that obligation just fine over the next couple of hours, that is, until the back right tire blows.

Dillon

"It is strange how new and unexpected conditions bring
out unguessed ability to meet them."
—Edgar Rice Burroughs, *The Warlord of Mars*

I HEAR MYSELF scream and wonder for a moment
if it's coming from someone else. And then I realize that
we've blown a tire. I grab the door handle, praying our
seatbelts hold while Klein fights for control of the car. It
is an utter miracle that he manages to get us into the side
lane without flipping the car. We *kathump* to a stop, and
both of us sit for a full few seconds with our heads pressed
against the seat backs, dragging in deep breaths of air.

"Did we run over something?" I ask.

"I never saw anything," Klein says, "but it's not out of
the realm of possibility."

"I'm hoping we have a spare," I say.

"Let me get out and check the back." He walks around

to the rear of the car, popping the trunk. I hear him say, "Yep, we have a spare."

"And I'm hoping you know how to change it," I call out through the lowered window.

"It's been a while," he says, "but here's hoping."

I get out of the car and walk around to the side, hoping none of the vehicles blowing past at eighty miles per hour decide to veer off the road and run into us. "Can I just say what an amazing job you did getting us to a stop?"

"Yeah, I'm thinking right now I will definitely continue with the weightlifting because that took about all the strength I have."

"Thank you then, for making the very wise decision to lift weights."

He smiles and shakes his head. "Now, to see if I can remember how to change a tire." He finds a jack in the trunk and carries the tire around to set it beside the blown one. It's literally in shreds, and I'm again amazed that we didn't wreck.

"Is there anything I can do to help?" I ask.

"Maybe just stand at the back of the car and make sure no one plows into us. If you see someone coming, make a dive for the grass over there, and I'll be right behind you."

I smile a little and say, "I'm really hoping that scenario doesn't play out. Although I have to admit I did see a news report before I left home about this car that ran out of gas. A police officer stopped to help her. While they were standing there, a huge truck lost control and ran right into them. Luckily, they were able to leap out of the way in time."

"Okay," Klein says, working a little faster now. "That's definitely making me want to get this done quick."

"I'm sorry," she says. "It just, well, it actually really did happen. I'm going to stop talking now."

I keep my eye on the traffic, but, admittedly, glance a few times at Klein, who is working at a pace that makes the muscles in his arms leap and dance beneath the skin. Not for the first time, I think what an incredible body he has. But then, that is not what I should be thinking about right now.

"I almost have it," Klein says. "Just a couple more minutes, and we should be out of here."

"Do you think maybe we picked a car that had a bad luck curse or something? I mean, we started with the muffler, and then there's the tire," I say.

"Maybe this will be the last of it," Klein says.

"Let's hope," I agree. Klein is true to his word, and within a few minutes, we're back inside the car and using the side lane as a ramp back onto the Autoroute.

We've been driving for about three hours when I say, "I'm actually famished. Would you want to stop at the next little town and get some lunch?"

"Sure," Klein says. "See anything on the map that looks good?"

"As a matter of fact, there's something that looks great just a few minutes ahead."

"Perfect," Klein says.

Fortunately, we spot the exit and get off the highway, winding around a curvy road that leads us to a charming little town whose buildings were all erected in centuries past. "This is beautiful," I say. "The thing about Europe is, you really can go town to town and be amazed by what's beautiful and unique in each place. And they all have something because there's such a wealth of history."

"To be honest," Klein says, "I never really thought much about coming to Europe. It wasn't something I had any real desire to do, but I understand now why people love coming here."

"We could park at the edge of town, and walk, see what we find," I suggest.

"That sounds good." He finds the first available spot to leave the car. My French is good enough to know that we don't need to put money in a meter or pay anyone. We start walking, and it isn't long before the first shops start to appear, first a bakery, whose window display makes my mouth literally water.

"Can you believe how beautiful their food is?" The bread is poofy and delicious looking. Desserts made of apple tarts, and beignets decorate beautiful wooden trays.

"We could get something from here on the way back out to take with us," Klein says.

"That sounds like a great idea," I agree. We walk on, passing an art gallery with lovely colorful canvas paintings adorning the walls, and it isn't long before we come to a cluster of cafés with outdoor seating. It's a beautiful sunny day, so we opt to sit outside and peruse the menu as soon as the waitress brings it to us.

"I have no idea what to order. I want everything on here," I say.

Klein laughs softly. "Me, too, but I think I'll go for the mushroom risotto."

"That sounds incredible. And I'm going to have the pizza and mashed potatoes."

Klein looks up at me and smiles. "Interesting combination."

"Gotta eat what you love," I say. "But let me qualify that with, both of those will be a treat. I try to stick to my mostly fruit and vegetable diet, which I actually love. It's not a hardship. But I do like to treat myself in places like this."

"And you should," Klein says. "Besides, you look amazing."

I feel the heat creep into my cheeks and glance down at the menu. "Thank you," I say.

"Am I right when I suspect that's hard for you to believe?"

"Hmm." I lift my shoulders in a shrug. "If I compared

myself to the women you most assuredly have throwing themselves at you on a regular basis, then, yeah, maybe."

He looks up at me then, meets my gaze and holds it directly. "I'm not interested in any of those women, though," Klein says.

We look at each other for several long moments, and I can feel my heart thudding against the wall of my chest, realize too that my cheeks have heated up again.

We finish our lunch and consider seeing more of the town but decide to get back on the road so that we can reach the château by dinner. An awkwardness has settled over us, and we drive for a bit without actual conversation beyond what is necessary to stay on top of our directions. At some point, I decide it might be a good idea to get things away from the personal and more on the reason behind the two of us setting out on this trip together.

I reach into the backpack at my feet and pull out a notepad and a pen. "Why don't we work on some song ideas?"

"Okay," he agrees. And I think that's relief I hear in his voice. I'm guessing the awkwardness between us was starting to bother him, too. So I decide to tackle that head-on. "I realize that the two of us, we're just, we're friends. And I'm not thinking this is about anything other than exactly what we agreed to. The two of us taking a little time to see the sights and write some songs. I know things got a little personal back there in the restaurant, and I don't want you to feel like—"

"Dillon." He says my name, and I stop. "I'm not thinking anything other than the fact that the last few days with you have been some of the best I've had in a long time. Whatever happens between us—" He hesitates and then, "I don't have any expectations. I just would kind of like to go on doing what we've been doing, enjoying life as we're living it right now in this moment. Nothing more, nothing less. Deal?"

"Deal."

Klein

"But how could you live and have no story to tell?"
—**Fyodor Dostoevsky,** *White Nights*

THE LAST THREE hours of the drive go by in a blink. I didn't know it would be possible to drive and write a song at the same time, but all Dillon has required of me is to think out loud. I seem to be able to do that and drive at the same time. We've ended up with some pretty incredible lyrics and have honed out a melody for most of the song except the final bridge.

"You're a productive person, aren't you?" I say, glancing at her as she taps out the melody with her fingers on the dashboard.

She shrugs a little. "I like to make use of my time. I also don't like to be bored. My brain prefers to be occupied."

"Mine, too, actually," I say. "I guess maybe that's the creative in us."

"When I'm in Nashville," she says, "and I have any amount of drive time, I use a recorder on my phone to dictate ideas and lyrics. It actually turns dead time into really productive time."

"That's admirable," I say. "No wonder you got songwriter of the year."

"I've written as much bad stuff as I have good," she says. "But I like to think that if you sift through the sand often enough, you'll find a gold nugget here and there."

"How many songs have you written?"

"Hmm, hundreds, I would say."

"And how many do you consider great?"

"We all like to think our creations are perfect, but I know better. A very small percentage of those songs are really good. An even smaller percentage would I call great."

"That's honest. I learned early on that just because I created something, it didn't mean that anyone else would find it worthwhile. It was only when I started looking outside myself to the way other people saw the world and tried to sync that with my own experience that I started to write things that might endure."

"When I first started performing, I didn't really care what a song had to say as long as it made people dance or raise their beers when I came on stage. Somewhere along the way, though, I realized it was kind of like I was throwing cotton candy at the crowd, and while they loved it in the moment, it wasn't anything that was going to stick with them very long or make them tell another person about the message in the song. I began to want to write and perform songs that would make them tell another person about it."

"Yeah, I get that," Dillon says. "I was kind of the same way in the beginning, looking at what other people were doing to try to figure out how to make it. But eventually, I figured out that the only story I can truly tell is my own story, bits and pieces of it, anyway, that resonate with other people and their stories. You have your own story that is unique to you, but there's so much of it that your fans are sure to identify with. It's finding those pieces of yourself that you would rather not show to the world and then realizing that other people feel the same about the things they believe are their flaws and weaknesses. We all have them. I think the reason people love music and books is because when a writer makes himself, herself vulnerable, the people listening to or reading that story understand that they're not alone, that they're not unique in their shortcomings."

I consider this for a moment. "That's true. It's just early on, it's hard to believe that people really want to see the ugly parts of you. I have a feeling," I say, glancing at her, "that you're going to make me open a vein and bleed whenever we write together."

"I won't consider this a success unless you do," she says, smiling.

The GPS announces our exit as upcoming. We put our attention on the road and not missing the turnoff to the château. Off the Autoroute, we drive a few miles south and then come to the château's massive stone column entrance. It has a gate we received the code for through a welcoming email.

Once we drive through, it's as if we've entered a movie set in the French countryside. To either side of us, beautiful green fields lie behind white-painted wood fencing. The pastures are dotted with grazing horses, a couple of which stand beneath trees along the edges of the fields. Others nap in the waning sunlight, tails swishing lazily. The road serving as the entrance goes on for at least half a mile. We round a turn. The château is there before us, an enormous stone monument to centuries past that has been lovingly maintained and cared for. Large boxwoods line the front of the house.

"They must be hundreds of years old," Dillon says. "They're huge."

To the right of the house, we can see the corner of a huge barn, white fencing that matches that along the driveway coming in.

"It's like we've stepped back in time or something," Dillon says.

A very discreet sign indicates parking to the left of the

château. I follow the drive around and pull in beside a few other vehicles. We get out and grab our suitcases from the trunk. I offer to take Dillon's, but she says, "Oh, it's easy. It's the pull kind."

We walk through the massive front door and into an area that serves as the lobby with several large sofas for seating. The front desk is to the right.

A smiling woman with gray hair and bright green eyes greets us with a sincere welcome. "We are so happy to have you," she says. "We will just check you in, and then I will be happy to show you to your room."

I hand her a credit card. Dillon reaches for hers. "It's fine," I say. "We'll settle up later."

"Are you sure?"

"Yes," I say.

We take care of the necessary paperwork, and then the woman helping us says, "Right this way, please. I will show you to your rooms. Your luggage will be up shortly."

We take the elevator to the second floor, and she leads us down a long, vast corridor.

"Here we are," she says, taking out a key, the old-fashioned kind instead of the card system hotels use today. "We have you in this room and then also the corner room. They are adjoining if you would like for me to open the door in between."

I look at Dillon, who looks at me, and we both say at the same time, "Oh, sure, of course, that'll be fine."

The woman gives us an odd look, as if she's trying to figure out exactly what we are to each other.

Neither of us decides to elaborate, and we are silent as she opens both rooms and points out the minibar. "Would you like ice brought to the room?"

"I think we're good," I say.

"Very well, then. I shall leave you to relax. I hope you will take time to explore the grounds a bit before it is dark. Are you having dinner in the château this evening?"

"Um, would you like to do that, Dillon?" I ask.

"Sure," she says.

"I'd be happy to make the reservation if you can tell me what time you would like to eat."

"Maybe eight o'clock?" I say.

"Yes," Dillon agrees. "That sounds great."

"Very well, it is done. Again, welcome to the château. Please do not hesitate to call the front desk if you need anything."

Once she leaves, the door clicking silently shut behind her, we turn to look at each other, the awkwardness we had felt during lunch today clearly ascending again.

"If you're more comfortable," I say, "we can shut the door between the rooms."

"Of course not," Dillon says, smiling. "You are the guy I shared a bed with one night, aren't you?"

I smile. "I believe I am that same guy."

"Okay then," she says lightly, "no secrets to hide from you."

"Would you like to walk around and check the place out before we get ready for dinner?"

"I would love to do that. This place is like a puzzle I can't wait to solve."

As soon as our suitcases arrive, we leave the room and head for the elevator and back to the main lobby. We find a brochure at the front desk that provides a layout of the property.

"I don't think we'll cover the whole thing before dinner," I say. "Which way do you want to go first?"

The woman who showed us to our rooms overhears our conversation and says from the front desk, "If I may recommend the lane to the left of the château. It will lead you to the orchard at the back of the property. The sunset from there is very beautiful."

"Sound good?" I ask, looking at Dillon.

"Yes, perfect."

We thank the woman and leave through the front of the château and then follow the map toward the recommended lane. In the distance, we can see a grove of trees.

"That must be the orchard," Dillon says. "Oh, I wonder if the trees have peaches on them."

"Let's go look," I say, and we head that way.

It takes us ten minutes or so to reach the edge of the

orchard, and sure enough, the trees are heavy with fruit not yet ripe.

"That has to be what heaven will smell like."

"It's wonderful," I agree.

We wind our way through the rows of trees, and it's a little magical witnessing the beauty of the fruit.

"It's a miracle, don't you think?" Dillon says. "How much fruit one tree can bear. Do you ever wonder why there's hunger in the world when we can grow things like this?"

"I think that's more of a people problem," I say, "than God not giving us enough tools for food."

"That's sad, isn't it?"

"Yes, it is," I say. "But then most things in this world are people problems."

We walk on a while longer, quiet as we simply take in the beauty of the place.

Dillon breaks the silence first. "It's so easy to think that our own little piece of the world is the best there is and that there's no need to see other places, but that really isn't true, is it? There's so much to see in this world and so many wonderful things we miss if we don't venture out."

"It does take some courage, though. I think that's why a lot of people don't leave what they know. It's risky, scary."

"True," Dillon says, "but the most rewarding things in life come with a little risk, don't they?"

We've stopped under one of the trees most heavily

loaded with fruit. Dillon turns to face me, and suddenly we're caught in a stare of awareness. The sun is setting behind us, pink rays of light streaming through the tree branches, darkening the color of the fruit even more. I realize how very much I want to kiss Dillon in that moment, and I can see that she sees this on my face. Her lips part, and she says my name, softly. I take the invitation I hear in her voice and lean in, down, down until my mouth finds hers. We kiss for a long, drawn-out time, and she tastes every bit as sweet as I imagine the fruit on the trees around us will taste when they're fully ripe.

When I finally pull back, I feel how much she wants me to continue. But I lift my head and blow out a rush of air.

"We should stop," I say.

"Should we?" she asks, her voice teasing and serious all at the same time.

"Not because I want to," I say.

"Why, then?"

"Because there will come a point not too far into this where stopping will feel like it's not an option."

"And if I said I don't want you to stop?" she asks softly.

"Hmm." I make a low sound in my throat and reach for her hand. "Come on, we've got some exploring left to finish."

I start to run then, pulling her along behind me. It would take only another word of protest from her, and I would stop right where we are and finish what we started.

Dillon

"Now a soft kiss – Aye, by that kiss, I vow an endless
bliss."
—John Keats

I TAKE EXTRA care getting ready for dinner,
spending quite a few extra minutes in the shower,
shampooing my hair, conditioning it, and then blow-
drying it straight once I'm out. I spend extra time with
my makeup, too, not wanting it to be so heavy as to be
noticeable, but hoping I have succeeded in smoothing out
my skin's imperfections and giving myself more eyelashes
than I was born with. I wear the basic black dress I had
brought with me. It's sleeveless and hits at mid-thigh, the
neckline simple. I hope it's elegant instead of too plain, but
it's the kind of thing I'm most comfortable in.

I throw on a pair of low-heeled sandals, add a spritz of
perfume and knock on the adjoining door between our
rooms.

"Come in," Klein calls out.

"Hey," I say, feeling my eyes widen a bit at the sight of him. He looks gorgeous. He's wearing jeans and a white-collar shirt with a navy blazer. "This too formal?"

"No. You look great."

"Thanks. You look amazing," he says, taking me in with eyes that clearly remember our kissing in the orchard a couple of hours ago. But then I'm remembering, too.

"Right then," he says. "Should we head on down to the restaurant?"

"Ready when you are."

We take the long corridor to the stairs, walking side by side, our hands close, but not touching. It's not difficult to find the restaurant from the main lobby. The smells lead us straight to it. A young woman at the entrance greets us with a welcoming smile. "Welcome," she says. "You have a reservation?"

"Yes," Klein says. "I'm not sure whose name it was put under, but either Matthews or Blake."

"Ah, yes, Mr. Matthews, we are so happy to have you." She pulls two menus from the back of the stand beside her and says, "Follow me, please."

The dining area is an enormous room overlooking the backside of the château. A stone terrace is visible from glass doors. Tables are strategically arranged around the room to somehow make the vast area seem cozy. Each table has a warmly lit lamp at its center. There are several other guests already dining. The hostess leads us to a table for two in a corner of the room. "Your waitress will be with you in just a few moments. Please do enjoy your evening," she says.

The waitress arrives within a few seconds, smiling a welcoming smile and handing us each a menu. She makes small talk in admirable English, telling us about a few of the feature specials for the evening. We listen intently, and when she gives us a few minutes to consider the options and leaves the table, Klein looks at me and says, "This is going to be a tough one."

"I know. Everything sounds wonderful."

In the end, when she returns to take our order, we both ask for versions of our various choices, me an assorted vegetable plate, Klein a delicious-sounding risotto dish. When he suggests that I order some wine if I would like, I decline. "I don't need it," I say.

"I don't want you to feel like you can't drink around me," he says. "I understand that other people can have a casual glass of wine, and that's all it is, and I'm fine with that."

"It's okay," I say. "When you're with intoxicating company, who needs it?"

He laughs outright at this, and I roll my eyes at my own bad joke. "Sorry," I say.

"No, I'm happy to be thought of as intoxicating," he says.

We opt for a bottle of sparkling water with lime instead,

and I don't know if it's the bubbles or my own ridiculous level of happiness that makes me realize yet again that I do not need alcohol to be completely happy around him. Talking with Klein is so easy. We drift from one topic of conversation to another, the seams in between as smooth and fluid as if we have known each other all our lives.

At one point, I question this. "Why is it so easy to talk to you? I mean, I know we have a lot in common, the music business, of course, but I don't know," I say, lifting my shoulders, "it just seems like I've known you forever."

He looks at me for a long, drawn-out moment and then says, "That makes me happy to hear that, Dillon. I actually don't have a lot of close friends. I'm glad to know that you and I have that."

His words should buoy me into another level of happiness, and, in a way they do. I wonder, though, if he wants me to know that friendship is all that he has in mind. So what if it is? I can certainly use a friend in my life. Truthfully, neither of us is in a place to consider more. I think about that kiss earlier this afternoon and wonder if he's regretting it or what it might have implied to me.

I decide to let him know he doesn't need to worry about that. "We all need friends, Klein. I know I do, and if you're thinking that I'm assuming we might be more than that because of this afternoon—"

"Dillon," he says, quietly interrupting me, "I loved what happened between us this afternoon. But my life is kind of a mess right now. Honestly, you don't deserve to be pulled into something I haven't even gotten figured out yet."

"It's okay," I say. "My life is pretty screwed up right at the moment. It would be wrong of me to let you think I am in a place—"

"I don't," he says, gently cutting me off. "I'm happy to live whatever this is in the moment. I sure didn't expect to come to Paris and end up doing this with you. But it's been one of those unexpected pleasures I will always be grateful for."

Somehow I think I hear a gentle letdown in this, but decide that the right thing to do is enjoy what we have here and now for what it is, without expecting it to ever be anything more. "That's exactly how I feel."

We finish the remainder of dinner under a new haze of weariness. Maybe it's just that both of us have decided we don't want to be the one to break this unspoken path of neutrality, but somehow throughout the remainder of the meal, our conversation feels stilted, as if we're back at a point of two people not really knowing each other, and so finding little to talk about.

We opt out of dessert, and when the waitress brings the check, Klein insists on paying it. I start to argue, but decide I'll just get the next meal. We walk back to the room, mostly quiet, except for a few impersonal comments on the château and its furnishings.

When we reach the room doors at the end of the hall,

we pause awkwardly. I pull my key from the small clutch purse I'd carried to dinner, wave it a little, and say, "Okay then, I'm really tired. I'm sure you are, too. So see you in the morning."

"Yeah," he says, "I'll see you in the morning." He pulls out his key and inserts it in the door, swinging it in and stepping into the room, closing it quietly behind him.

I step inside my own room then and close the door, leaning against it with my head resting on the wood. I shut my eyes and wonder exactly what just happened. Did I misread something? Say too much? I don't know, but no point in trying to fix it now.

A knock sounds on the door that connects our rooms. I startle in a moment of surprise, take a deep breath, and walk over to open it.

Klein is standing there looking at me, not as he had in the hallway a few moments ago, but as he had looked at me this afternoon in the orchard. Something warm and happy unfurls in the center of my chest, and I bite my lip, heart thumping hard. We don't say a word.

He merely ducks in, his hands anchored on my waist, lifting me up and carrying me back against the wall behind us. I wrap my legs around him, my arms around his neck. He kisses me. All reserve gone now, we devour each other. Any of the doubts we voiced to this point have dissipated like dust in the wind.

The truth is, I don't want to think about anything except

how amazingly good it feels to be in the arms of a man who clearly wants me, a man I cannot deny wanting more than I have ever wanted anyone in my life. I don't bother trying to hide this from him. I kiss him back with complete abandon. My fingers find the top button of his shirt, undo it. I hear his quick intake of breath, feeling a sharp stab of pleasure for the realization that I can make him respond this way. I don't even know how long we kiss like this before his hands find the zipper of my dress, slide it down tentatively as if a question is attached to the action.

I make a sound that lets him know it is exactly what I want. The zipper slides to its end, and he slowly, carefully, lowers the shoulders of my dress down my arms where it stops at my waist. He drops his gaze to my breasts, mostly hidden behind a black lacy bra. The old self-consciousness grips me, but I realize in that moment that no one has ever looked at me with such longing, such desire. I drop my head back in invitation. His mouth finds my neck, kissing his way down to the top of my left breast. I can barely breathe at this point, afraid that if I do so, he will stop, take it as some audible sign that I want him to, but nothing could be further from the truth.

But then again, I'm thinking of the times I had nearly thrown myself at Josh, how clear it had been that at some point he had stopped wanting me, and I stiffen unintentionally.

"What is it?" Klein asks, pulling back to look down at me, his hand at the side of my neck.

"I'm sorry," I say. "It's not you. It's just me thinking about how awful things with Josh got, and how there was a time when they weren't like that."

"Hey. I'm not Josh, and I can't even begin to imagine what he was thinking. I mean, to have a woman like you and—"

"Don't," I say, mentally flinching a little. "I didn't say that to make you feel sorry for me."

"Sorry is the last thing I feel for you," he says softly. "Have I not made that clear enough?"

I force myself back to the present, leaving the memories where they belong, in the past. I look up at him, and I cannot deny that this thing happening between us feels very, very real.

"I'm sorry," I say. "I didn't mean to bring all that baggage into this."

"It's okay." He takes a defining step back. "But I think it's probably a good idea if I say good night."

"That's really the last thing I want you to say," I admit.

He leans in, kisses me deep and full, and then with a sigh of resignation, says, "I'm going now, back to the other room, closing the door between us. I very strongly suggest that you lock it."

I reach out to put a hand on his arm in protest, making

a sound of disappointment. But I know that he's right, and so I let him go.

Klein

"Monitor motives."

—Daren Martin

I AM AWAKE WITH the sun and unable to go back to sleep. I decide to go outside and take a walk in the early morning fresh air. I leave through the massive front door of the château, grabbing a cup of coffee made available for guests. The steaming cup is warm in my hands, and I take a sip, enjoying the robust taste of the French coffee.

The sun is rising on the horizon of a beautiful green field to my left. I follow the path we had taken yesterday to the orchard, breathing in the sweet scent of the fruit I can smell even from this distance away. I nearly finish the coffee by the time I reach the orchard's edge, and I take the last sip, pressing the paper cup together and sticking it in my jacket pocket.

My phone dings, and I consider ignoring it, reluctant to let its intrusion into the peace here affect me. But there's always that worry that something is wrong somewhere. So I glance at the screen, tap into my message app. It's from Riley.

Hey, I'm sure you're not up yet, and it's late here, but I was thinking about you and just wanted to see how you're doing. Make sure you're keeping up all your healthy habits, vitamins and such. You know, I really admire your discipline and dedication to stay healthy now that you've got that back again. Anyway, we may not be together anymore, but I do still care about you.

I swipe out of the app, tuck my phone into the other pocket of my jacket and walk on into the orchard. My steps faster now. I'm surprised to hear from Riley, given our last communication. Why she considers it her mission to keep me healthy, I don't know. Something about the message bothers me in a way I can't explain. I guess it's just an ex-girlfriend letting me know she still cares about me. Nothing horrible about that, but I know Riley, and there is always a purpose to everything she does. It's just who she is. It took me a long time to figure that out, but once I did, I found myself always questioning her motives.

I think of our baby, and a rise of grief swoops through me. I wonder if it will ever not feel this way. I don't think so. It doesn't matter that I never met our baby. Never even saw him or her. This loss I feel is the same as if I had held the baby in my arms.

I walk to the far end of the orchard, letting the pureness of this place infuse me with a desire not to go to the deep dark place. Not letting thoughts of Riley ruin the start to a beautiful day. I think of the place I had been in when I arrived in Paris, of how I had absolutely no desire to continue the career I had thought was everything I wanted in life. I honestly don't know if that's true anymore or not, but something about these last few days with Dillon has made me want to care again. To know what I want to come next. And even though I don't have an answer for that right now, I at least have the desire to try and figure it out.

Dillon

"One cannot think well, love well, sleep well, if one has
not dined well."
—**Virginia Woolf,** *A Room of One's Own*

I WAKE TO sunlight streaming into the room. I hadn't
bothered to close the curtains last night. As I have done my
entire life, I wake to the light. I slide out of bed, deciding
to call room service for a pot of coffee before I get in the
shower. When it arrives, my hair is still wet. I answer the
door to a kind-faced older man holding a silver tray.

"Bonjour, madame," he says.

"Good morning," I say and step aside to let him in. He
places the tray on the corner of the bed and leaves with a
polite wish that I have a good day.

I pour myself a cup and take a gratifying sip, wondering
if Klein is up yet. I haven't heard anything from the other
room, so I decide maybe not, take my cup into the

bathroom and dry my hair. Once I'm ready, I decide to go downstairs and see what there is to do during the day here. Just as I step out the door, I see Klein walking down the long hallway.

"Good morning," I say, suddenly awkward with memories of last night.

"Good morning," he says. "How did you sleep?"

"Great," I say. "You look like you've been up a while."

"I have, actually. I decided to take a walk down to the orchard again. It's incredibly beautiful there."

"It is," I say. "Do you want to get some breakfast?"

"Sure. I had a little coffee earlier, but I'm starving."

We turn then and head downstairs to the restaurant where we'd had dinner last night. A different waitress leads us to a table, this time close to the terrace doors where we can appreciate the view of the enormous lawn off the stone terrace.

The smells coming from the kitchen are genuinely mouthwatering, and I open my menu. "Do you think they would bring me one of everything on here?"

"It is tempting, isn't it?" Klein says.

We place our order within a couple of minutes. I decide to splurge on the blueberry pancakes. Klein opts for an omelet. The waitress brings us a mouthwatering basket of pastries that appear to have been made in the château kitchen. We both dig in as if we haven't eaten in a week, and I force myself to stop after the second croissant. "I'm not going to have any room for blueberry pancakes," I say.

"If I stayed here too long," Klein says, "I'm pretty sure I would put on twenty pounds."

"Do you ever wonder why the French people aren't fat?" I ask.

"Actually, I have wondered," Klein says. "I did a google search on that when we were in Paris, because it occurred to me that if you just went by the foods they eat, they should be, but they're not."

"Fast food isn't on every corner, for one thing," I say.

"Yeah," he agrees. "Definitely that. And then there's the fact that people here tend to walk more every day than Americans in general. Then there's the whole red wine thing."

"Resveratrol," I say.

"Did you google the same article?"

I laugh lightly. "No, but I've read a few things here and there about the topic. Snack foods don't seem to be as prevalent here. It seems like people emphasize meals and sitting down to eat more, whereas the American lifestyle is a little more about rushing here and there and eating fast food to go in the car. At least I'm guilty of that."

"I think we all are more than we should be," Klein says. "But I'm going to try to make one of my takeaways from this trip, making some changes on all of that."

"Me, too."

Just then, the waitress brings our breakfast, and despite having eaten bread in advance, I still cannot resist my blueberry pancakes. "This may be the best thing I've ever eaten," I say, looking at Klein with a smile of pleasure. "Would you like a bite?"

"Actually, I would. I'm having a pretty serious case of pancake envy."

I laugh, pick up a clean fork, and hand him a bite. "There you go," I say.

"That is amazing," he says, savoring it.

"Yes, I'm sure I will be wearing it for the rest of the vacation," I say, deliberately putting down my fork. "I think I've exceeded my carb quota for the day. In fact," I say, "I could use some serious activity today. What do you think?"

"What do they offer?" Klein asks.

"I was looking at a brochure in the room, and they do offer riding."

"Remember I said I've never been on a horse before?"

"I do, but there's a first time for everything."

"And what if I'm a complete failure at it?"

"We'll just walk," I say. "Go for a nice ride out through the countryside. Doesn't that sound wonderful?"

"I guess I'll be a sport and give it a shot."

"Great," I say, excited. "Because it's been a lot of years since I've been on a horse, but I can't think of a more beautiful place to ride. You will love it," I assure him.

"Promise?" he says.

"I promise."

Dillon

"When you are on a great horse, you have the best seat
you will ever have."
—**Winston S. Churchill**

OF COURSE, NEITHER of us has riding clothes, so
after a quick call to the front desk, we opt for jeans. They
have a slot open at ten o'clock, so just after nine-thirty, we
leave the château and walk down the path that leads to the
stables. Like the château, the barn here is designed to make
you feel like you've stepped back in time. It's spotless and
neat, the wood features newly stained and varnished, all
the metal recently painted black as well.

We step inside the main entrance located at the middle
of the barn. A long aisle reaches end to end, stalls on either
side. Most of the horses appear to be outside, but a few
heads pop over the stall doors at the sight of us. A horse
whinnies, and I wish I had thought to bring some kind of
treat with us.

"Hello, there." A young man in a bill cap approaches us. "You must be Dillon and Klein. I am André. I have you down for a ride this morning."

"Yes," I say.

"So have either of you ever ridden before?"

"I have," I say. "Just kind of backyard stuff."

He turns to Klein. "And how about you?"

"No, actually, I never have."

"Then you are in for a nice time," he says. "The horses here are really pets and love their life, so we'll have a beautiful ride out through the vineyard and then back around by the orchard. You chose a beautiful day for it."

"Will there be anyone else on the ride?" Klein asks.

"You are my only two guests this morning."

"Oh, okay," Klein says, and I can tell that he is relieved.

"Follow me, and I'll introduce you to your equine companion for the day." We walk behind him down one length of the aisle to a pair of grooming stalls, where two horses stand waiting for us. They've already been tacked up except for their bridles, standing quietly in the crossties attached to their halters. "This is Samuel," André indicates, patting a hand on the black horse's shoulder.

"He is a charmer this one and will do his best to clear you of any peppermints you might have in your pocket. Speaking of which, I'll give you some inventory." He reaches for a jar to the side of one of the stalls, hands me a few, and Klein as well.

We stick them inside the pockets of our jeans, and at the sound of the crinkle, both horses perk up their ears. "Is it all right if they have one?" I ask.

"Of course," André says.

We both unwrap one and give it to each horse. "The chestnut here is Abby, and given the size ratio, I would say she's probably a better fit for you, Dillon. Klein, you can have the big boy here."

Another young helper appears, smiles a greeting at us, and then sets about putting the bridles on the horses. Once he's done, he leads them out of the grooming stalls and down the aisle toward a mounting block at the far entrance.

"I will get my horse and meet you out there in just a moment," André says.

Klein and I follow the young assistant to the mounting block. He indicates that I should get on Abby first, so I do, my heart thumping a little in anticipation since it's been so long since I've been on a horse. But Abby stands patiently, ignoring my awkwardness, and once I'm in the saddle, she steps forward a few steps, obviously knowing the routine as the assistant leads the other horse to the mounting block.

Klein looks more than a little doubtful at this point, but following his intention to be a good sport, he steps up and follows the assistant's instructions. "So," the young man says. "You will put your left foot in the stirrup and swing your weight up and over the horse as gently as possible and then put your foot in the other stirrup. Any questions?"

"Ah, no, I don't think so," Klein says, glancing up at me. I smile reassuringly and watch as he executes a perfect swing into the saddle, easing his weight onto the horse's back.

"Are you sure you've never done this before?" I ask, smiling.

He looks up and shakes his head. "I assure you, no. I have not."

The assistant then shows him how to hold the reins, and we wait a moment before André appears around the corner of the barn, riding a beautiful white horse. "This is Zeus," he says. "Are we all ready to go?"

"I think so," Klein says, and I nod in agreement, patting my horse's neck.

"You can follow me then. To ask your horse to go forward, just give a little squeeze with your calves and keep your fingers loose on the reins. If you want to stop, just give a gentle squeeze on the reins. You really don't need to pull back on them."

Klein thanks the assistant for his help, and then we're off, following single file down the lane leading away from the barn. The scenery is absolutely breathtaking, like something out of a movie, really. Klein is behind me, and I look back now and then to see him relaxed to the point that he is starting to enjoy the scenery as well.

We ride for fifteen or twenty minutes through a valley of sorts, beautiful old green trees on either side of us. We reach a knoll at one point, and then to our left, I spot the vineyard. Rows and rows of grapevines loaded with fruit stretching out before us. I glance back to see Klein taking it in as well and say, "The smell is amazing."

"Yes," André says, glancing back. "The estate makes its wine from this very vineyard. The grapevines here are at least a century old."

"Has the château been in the same family from its beginning?"

"Actually, yes," André says. "It has. My parents are the most recent owners of the estate."

"Oh," I say. "How wonderful. You are very lucky."

"Yes, I think so," he says. "I have traveled to many other places during my life so far, and I always want to come back here."

"That's the thing about home, isn't it?" I say.

"Yes, it is," he says.

A few flies have started to appear, landing on the horses' necks and hindquarters. They swish their tails and shake their heads to make them go away. "How is it that you found us?" André asks, glancing back at Klein.

"Dillon found you through a Google search, actually," he says.

"And I'm so glad that we were able to come," I say.

"What is it that you two do when you're not in France?" André asks.

"Music," Klein says.

"Ah. What kind of music?"

"Country," Klein says.

"Do you write, sing?"

"Klein sings," I say. "He's being modest, actually. He's a pretty well-known country music star."

Klein starts to shrug that off, when André says, "Really? I love country music. I was in Nashville last year. You are Klein Matthews," he says suddenly, making the connection.

I smile, while Klein looks a bit uncomfortable. "Yes," he says.

"Amazing," André says. "I listened to your music when I was in your country and put it on my Spotify playlist."

"Thank you," Klein says. "That's actually very nice to hear. And while we're busy handing out accolades, Dillon here is a very well-known songwriter in the country music industry."

André sends me a smile and says, "Incredible that the two of you found us here, and I am now such a country music fan. You played in Paris recently, didn't you?"

"Yes," Klein says. "Actually, that's how I ended up in France."

"Lucky for us," André says. "Will you be staying at the château tonight?"

"Yes," I say.

"Then you must let me take you out to our most popular dance club. You would like to go?" he asks.

Klein glances at me, and I shrug and nod.

"Sure," Klein says. "That sounds like fun."

It is clear that we have made André's day, and he spends the next half hour or so of our ride giving us the history of the estate and telling us about his family members. We wind along through another valley until we reach the edge of the orchard. The smell of peaches is fragrant in the air.

We take our time heading back to the barn. I can see that Klein has thoroughly enjoyed himself. "So much for you not being able to ride," I say, with the barn just visible in the distance.

A whinny sounds from the field near the barn. We see a few horses start to prance around the pasture at the sight of us. Klein's horse raises his head, nickers back, and then starts to trot in place.

"Just sit back, Klein and take your reins," André says.

But the horse has other ideas, and all of a sudden, he leaps in the air and takes off at a gallop for the barn.

"Sit in the saddle, Klein! Sit back and take your reins!" André yells out.

Klein attempts to do so, but there's no stopping the horse now. He has decided he's going to the barn. I can only pray that Klein will be able to stay on.

The horse is going at a dead gallop, sending up clouds of

dust behind him so that it is difficult to make out whether or not Klein is still in the saddle. At André's direction, we trot along the path, trying to balance running after Klein's horse and making it go faster with getting to him as quickly as possible.

I literally feel sick thinking of how I had talked Klein into riding today. I imagine a dozen different horror scenarios in which Klein is being dragged along behind the horse, one foot still in the stirrup, or that he'll be bucked off into one of the nearby trees. We begin to catch up with them, though, and I can see that Klein is still in the saddle.

"Wrap your legs around the horse!" André yells again at the top of his voice, and I see Klein do precisely that. He's sitting in the saddle like someone who has been riding their entire life. My nausea starts to be replaced with pride for Klein's ability to handle something I am sure I would not have managed.

We're still pretty far back when I see the horse stop at the barn entrance. Klein reaches out and rubs the horse's neck. I am again filled with pride for his ability to not be angry at the horse.

We trot up behind them less than a minute later, and André says, "Thought you didn't know how to ride, Klein?"

Klein has climbed out of the saddle by now. He looks at both of us, shaking his head with a smile.

"Well, it's one of those things where you learn on the job, I guess."

We all laugh, even if mine is mostly in relief. But at some point in the not-too-distant future, it probably will be a funny story to tell.

The assistant from earlier appears to take the horse from Klein. Klein walks inside the barn, retrieves a couple of peppermints from the jar, and opens one to give his horse. He then walks over and hands one to me for mine.

"I'm so sorry," I say.

"Hey, I'm not," Klein says. "That's the most exciting thing that's happened to me in a long time, and I lived to tell about it. That's not too bad, huh?"

"You're pretty amazing, you know that?" I say. "You'd have every right to be hating me right now."

"Not me," he says, looking deep into my eyes. And for a moment, everything around us drops away, and it's just the two of us standing there taking each other in.

"Good job, man," André says, breaking the spell. "You two still up for some clubbing tonight?"

"More so than ever," Klein says.

"One thing has to be true," André says. "If you can ride like that, I know you can dance."

Klein

"Reject your sense of injury and the injury itself
disappears."
—Marcus Aurelius

WE HAVE A late lunch in the château restaurant, both
of us still full from breakfast, despite all the activity. Dillon
feels guilty for what had happened, but the truth of it is, I
haven't enjoyed myself that much in a very long time.

"Where did you learn to ride, Dillon?" I ask her once our
salads arrive.

"My grandpa had a farm when I was growing up. He
mostly raised cows, but when he discovered how much
I wanted a pony, he bought one for me, and whenever
I visited them on weekends or during the summer, that's
pretty much all I would do. I never had any formal lessons
or anything. I probably spent as much time falling off as
I did actually riding, but she was the cutest little pony.

247

I couldn't have been prouder of her had he bought me a fancy European imported horse. We weren't rich, my mama and I, but I have pretty wonderful memories of things I used to do on my grandparents' farm. He had this pond that he built and put some fish in. I would ride my pony out there on hot summer days and let her go in for a swim. She loved it so much, and I felt like the richest person in the world getting to do that with her."

"What happened to her?" I ask softly.

"She died when I was a senior in high school. She colicked one night, and no one found her until the next day. I felt so guilty because I had stopped going out there as much. I guess I felt like I had abandoned her."

"I'm sure no one else saw it that way. That's kind of what happens during those years. Things that had been so important before taking a backseat. But it's just the nature of growing up and trying to figure out how to make your way in the world."

Tears well in her eyes. She shakes her head as if to try and push the memories away.

"Hey," I say. "I'm sorry. I didn't mean to dredge up painful stuff."

"No, it's okay," she says. "It's just one of those regrets I have in life, and hopefully, I've tried to do better by the things I've loved since then."

"We all have regrets like that somewhere in our past, Dillon. You're not the only one."

I glance out the window toward the green expanse of lawn. "I was probably seven when my dad went to jail. He was really an abusive son of a bitch, but he was still my dad. I guess, honestly, I was happy and sad when they arrested him and put him in the back of the county sheriff's car. When it became clear that he wasn't going to be coming home any time soon, he sent word through my mom that he would like for me to come and visit him. She tried to get me to go on the days that she was sober, that is. And I knew that I should, but there was a part of me that really didn't want to. That was the part I went with. And so, on the night we got the call that he had died in his cell, I was probably eight by then. I realized I was never going to have the chance to redo that decision. At first, it seemed like it couldn't actually be true. And I wouldn't be honest if I didn't admit that some part of me felt glad that I would never have to deal with him again. But what eventually won out was regret, of course, that I hadn't gone to see him. It was the last thing he ever asked of me."

"You were just a little boy. How could you have known?"

"I couldn't have, but I didn't go because, truthfully, I hated him. It's something I've had to live with for the rest of my life, and sometimes I wonder what might have happened if I had gone. Would it have given him the will to turn away from the drugs and try to start over?"

"That's an awfully big burden of blame to put on

yourself," she says. "We're all responsible for the choices we make, and sad as it is, your dad's choices are what put him there."

"I know," I say. "There's absolutely no doubt about that, but I guess maybe I'd like to entertain the notion now and then that maybe he would have loved me enough to give it up."

"He should have loved you enough to give it up."

"Yeah," I say. "He should have."

I reach across the table and take his hand in mine. "Whatever his faults, Klein, he did a great thing by giving you to the world."

Riley

"The best laid schemes o' Mice an' Men,
Gang aft agley.
An' lea'e us nought but grief an' pain,
For promis'd joy!"
—**Robert Burns**

IRONICALLY, I AM writing an email to Klein when I feel the first pain slice through my midsection. It completely takes my breath away. I gasp, short and hard. I sit for a moment, wondering if it could be something I've eaten that upset my stomach and has nothing at all to do with the baby. I wait a full minute for the pain to recur, but it doesn't. I sit still for another full five minutes, finally breathing a sigh of relief when it doesn't happen again.

I glance at the screen of my laptop, reread the words I have written to Klein, an explanation of the truth about our baby.

I agonize for a bit over the inability I seem to have for

conveying the why behind my actions. But then I wonder if that really matters because I know one thing for sure. When Klein learns of the existence of this baby, he will be willing to forgive me anything. I guess, truthfully, that is all that matters.

It might just be that the one smart thing I've done is to pick a guy with a conscience, with a heart that always wants to do right. He will hate me at first. There's no denying this. But his relief at learning the truth will win out. Klein is a strong man. There's nothing soft about him when it comes to getting the things he's wanted in life, chasing after the career that defines him. But he and I are different in this one respect.

I'm willing to do whatever it takes to get the things I want in life. Klein has limits, morals, you might say. Places he's unwilling to go. A shimmer of pain ripples through me, but it's a shadow of the one from a few minutes ago. I close my eyes and wait, letting myself wonder for just a moment what will happen if I actually lose this baby.

I cannot imagine having to start over again, find another man who can give me the things I want. Just the thought is exhausting, and I vow anew to take care of this life inside me. I rub my belly, as if the baby can actually feel this. I resolve to eat better, get a book, and read up on whatever nutrients this baby needs. I will do all of that and more. I'm not sure if I'm making this promise to myself or a god I don't believe in. Either way, I will not let anything happen to this baby. I will not.

Dillon

"Let us read, and let us dance; these two amusements will never do any harm to the world."

—**Voltaire**

THE PLAN IS to meet André downstairs at eight. I had decided to take a nap, and it's nearly seven when I wake up in a panic. I jump into the shower, wash my hair, and do my fastest version of getting ready.

Klein knocks on the door between our rooms a little before eight. I pull it open to see him standing there looking hotter than ever in faded jeans and a white collared shirt.

"Hey," he says, "you look great."

"Thank you. I wasn't really sure what to wear," I say, running a hand across the short skirt I'd found at the bottom of my suitcase.

"I think you nailed it," he says, his gaze warm on mine. "Ready to head down?"

"Let me grab my purse."

I duck back into the room, throw a lipstick and my phone inside the clutch, and head for the door.

André is waiting for us downstairs. A young woman in her twenties stands next to him. André makes the introductions with a smile. "Elizabetta, these are my new friends, Klein and Dillon."

And to us, "Klein and Dillon, this is Elizabetta. She couldn't believe I met the two of you here, so I had to bring her along to prove it."

Elizabetta laughs a shy laugh. "Believe it or not, I had tickets for your concert in Paris, but my mother was in a little car accident, and I did not want to leave her until I knew she was okay."

"I'm sorry," Klein says. "I hope she is all right?"

"She is, thank you. But I thought André must be kidding me to say that you are here at the château. And you," Elizabetta says, looking at me, "you write songs?"

"I do," I say.

"That is amazing. We love music, André and I," Elizabetta says, waving a hand between them. "We will have so much fun tonight. Shall we go?"

We follow André and Elizabetta down the broad stone steps of the château entrance to a dark gray Range Rover waiting at the center of the drive. André thanks the valet who has pulled the vehicle to the front and gets in the driver's seat. Klein and I slide in the back, and then we're heading down the long drive that leads to the main road.

"The place where we are going," André says, "it will take thirty minutes or so, but the drive is beautiful during the day. At night you can't see as much, but I will still point out a few things of interest along the way."

It is clear as we go along that André loves his country and the town and surrounding countryside where he grew up. He regales us with stories from his childhood and some of the things he used to do as a boy with his parents and grandparents. We pass a wonderful-sounding farmers' market where the fruits and vegetables for the château restaurant are still bought today. And farther on, a beautiful, small stone church where his parents were married and the elementary and high schools he attended as a student.

"I understand why you always want to come back," Klein says. "We are in a different country, of course, but so much of what you've said reminds me of small towns in the United States."

"I love in country music," Elizabetta says, "how so many songs are stories of life in small towns. Did you grow up in a small town, Dillon?"

"Yes," I say, "actually, I did."

"Do you write about your life there?" Elizabetta asks.

"I have, and I still do draw on pieces of my childhood. It's very much a part of who I am."

"I have always wondered what it would be like to be a writer and tell stories that other people recognize something of themselves in."

"When we get it right, I think that's what happens. They're sort of like our children, though. We're reluctant to consider any of them inferior," I say with a smile.

"I am envious," Elizabetta says, "of your talent."

I start to shrug off the compliment, but I can see that she sincerely means it. And so, I simply say, "Thank you so much."

~

THE CLUB IS a renovated feed mill. The outside walls are stone and look centuries old, but the inside has been brought up to date with red leather chairs and booths, and a large dance floor. The bar is made with what looks like beautiful green sea glass. A copper glass rack dangles from above the bar. Multiple bartenders are busy making drinks. The music has a deep, throbbing beat, and for the first time in longer than I can remember, I really want to dance. I reach for Klein's hand, pull him toward the dance floor.

"Contrary to André's prediction, I'm not the greatest dancer," he leans in and says near my ear.

"Neither am I," I say. "Let's just have some fun."

And that is exactly what we do. For the next two hours or a little more, we are nonstop on the dance floor, the only thing pulling us off is a quick trip to the bar for sparkling water to quench our thirst.

It's somewhere after midnight when the DJ decides to slow things down. I instantly recognize the introductory notes of the song as one of Klein's. "Oh my gosh, it's yours!"

Klein looks over his shoulder at André, who is dancing nearby with Elizabetta. André waves a hand, letting us both know that he has requested the song. Klein looks a little uncomfortable, but then pulls me up close, one arm looped around my waist, and we settle into the twang of a Nashville steel guitar behind Klein's whiskey-smooth voice. It's a little surreal being somewhere in France dancing to one of the top country songs from last year, and in the arms of the artist singing it.

I rest my cheek against his chest, flowing in sync with the music, fueling the dancing of everyone around us. For a moment, I let myself wonder what it would be like to have Klein in my life. For him to be the man I have a right to dance with this way. I lean back, looking up at him, and I'm guessing my eyes must be revealing what I'm thinking because Klein dips his head and finds my mouth with his, kissing me full and deep. All my thoughts fall away, and there is nothing except this moment between us, the beat of the music, and I wish, truly wish, we could stay like this forever, that there wasn't real life waiting for us. Me, in the finality of an ugly divorce, Klein uncertain about his career and the ex-girlfriend whose choices haunt him.

For now, though, it's just this, and I tighten my arms

around his neck, kissing him back with no desire whatsoever to hide what I'm feeling. I want to give him all the emotion inside me, let him know there is nowhere else I want to be, no one else I want to be with. We both seem to forget there are other people around us.

For once, I don't care what anyone else thinks. I only care that Klein knows how much my time with him has meant, how I wish it didn't have to end. The song is fading into its final notes when he takes my hand and leads me across the dance floor through the hallway that leads to an exit. We make our way outside into the cool night air.

An ancient stone wall encircles the building that houses the club. Klein leads me to a darkened corner. I lean against the wall. He clamps his hands to my waist and lowers his head, his mouth finding mine, hungry, devouring in a way I have not yet felt from him. This feeling of being wanted is utterly intoxicating, and I loop my arms around his neck, pulling him as close as I can, pressing myself into him, wanting nothing more than to give every part of myself to him.

For a moment, a very brief moment, I remember what it felt like to wonder if I would ever feel attractive again, and that memory attempts to mar the happiness I feel here with Klein. But I refuse to let it, forcing it away from the present and banishing it to the past, where I know now that it belongs. We kiss for a very long time, the audible beat from the club music thumping around us. It mimics my heartbeat, and when Klein pulls away to look down at me, his voice is low and a little urgent when he says, "Why don't we catch our own ride back to the château? I really want you alone right now."

I can't bring myself to speak an answer, not trusting my voice. I simply nod, and leave no doubt to myself, or to Klein, that there is nothing I want more.

Klein

"Know that everything is in perfect order whether you
understand it or not."
—Valery Satterwhite

IT'S NEARLY TWO A.M. when we get back to the
château.

Dillon and I have said very little the last part of the drive,
but I hold her hand on the seat between us. I can feel
her pulse throbbing against my palm in perfect rhythm to
my own thudding heart. We walk through the lobby, our
fingers still entwined, an urgency in my steps now that I
can't deny. We take the long hallway to our rooms, stop in
front of my door. I look at Dillon without saying anything.
She reads my thoughts and simply says, "Yes."

I insert the key in the door, pull her in behind me. Once
the lock has clicked into place, I turn for her, my hands on
her waist, pulling her to me, our bodies flush against each
other. I hear her soft intake of breath and feel the way she

melts into me. She pulls me in and kisses me fully, with a desire that lights me up from the inside. I kiss her back, and we engage in a dance of back and forth, our hands no longer still but exploring, touching, pulling loose clothes, my shirt, the zipper of her skirt. I pull her blouse from her shoulders, unbuttoning as I go. I look down to take in the black lacy bra covering her breasts and then lower my mouth to graze the top of each beautiful swell.

"Dillon," I say, my voice low and hoarse. "I want you so much. I need you in a way I can't even understand myself."

She lifts my head with a fingertip beneath my chin, looks at me with a long, smoldering look, and says, "You have no idea how nice it is to hear that."

And I know the why behind her words, understand that this is something she needs to hear for reasons that don't apply to the moment. I'm glad that I can give that to her. But it is honest, and only comes from the fact that I find her not only undeniably beautiful but so many of the things I have never imagined finding in a woman altogether in one person.

"I know this isn't the right time for us," I say. "There are too many things unfinished in our real lives, but that doesn't change the fact that what we've found here between us is real, and I want it, Dillon."

And then she's kissing me again. We manage to rid ourselves of the remainder of our clothing. I stand for a moment, staring down at her with no attempt to hide how much I want her. She slides her hands up my chest, clasps them behind my neck. I savor the feel of her body against mine. I lean down and lift her up in my arms, carrying her to the bed, where I place her gently on to the mattress.

She lies back against the pillow, one arm thrown above her head, no longer self-conscious. I lower myself down beside her, stretch out so that our bodies are aligned. I raise up on one elbow, tracing a finger from the center of her forehead, down her nose, across her full lips, the tip of her chin, the hollow at the center of her neck. And then around each side of her breasts. She breathes soft and shallow now, and I know that she wants me as much as I want her. But I still need to ask. "Are you sure, Dillon, that this is what you want?"

"Yes," she says, adamant now.

But I can see the worry in her eyes, and say, "The last thing I would ever want to do is take advantage of you."

"You're not," she says. "I think if I let this night pass me by, I will never forgive myself."

I consider this for a moment, then lean down and kiss her with all of the longing inside me, and yet, I know this isn't the right time. That there will be a time for us somewhere ahead in the future. I don't know when or how. I just know that it will be. And that the right thing for tonight is to save what we both want so much for the time when we are free and clear. I am about to tell her this when my phone rings.

Dillon

"The high road is something very, very long, of which one cannot see the end – like human life, like human dreams. . .Vive la grande route and then as God wills."

—**Fyodor Dostoyevsky**

I WATCH AS KLEIN puts down the phone, realizing that something is terribly wrong. It's the middle of the night, and no call at this time ever heralds anything good. "What happened?" I ask, my voice a little more than a whisper. "Who was that?"

"Curtis, my manager," Klein says, sitting on the edge of the bed now, his back to me. He's quiet for several long seconds before he adds, "He said that Riley is at the hospital in labor—"

He stops there, but he doesn't need to finish the sentence. A wave of sickness washes over me. I sit up and slide to the edge of the bed, facing away from him now and reaching for my clothes. "The baby is yours," I say.

"I don't know how that can be," Klein says. "She told me she—"

"But she actually didn't."

"Why would she do that?" Klein says, his voice razor-edged with agony.

I'm not sure if he's asking the question of himself or of me. "I cannot imagine."

"I thought the choice that she made was her way of getting back at me, but was this actually it? For her to have the baby and not allow me to be involved?"

"I don't know," I say. "What are you going to do?"

"I have no idea."

"You have to go back," I say. "You have to go to the hospital."

He's quiet now, and I can feel his agreement. Even if he hasn't voiced it out loud, we both know that there is no other option. If the baby is his, and there seems to be little doubt, he needs to make his presence known now.

"You have to go," I say again.

He turns then to look at me, and I can see in his eyes regret for what is about to happen between us, and the realization, too, that our time here might have been all the time together we'll ever know.

"I'm sorry," he says. "This is not how I wanted this night to end."

"This is your baby. You have to be there."

"Yes," he says, standing. "When will you come back?"

"I'm not sure," I say, realizing I really have no idea. It's clear to me then that I haven't been thinking beyond our stay in France. It's as if I've been holding my breath, waiting to see what would happen and how that would affect where we went from here.

"Can I see you when you get back?" he asks.

I want to say yes. So very much. But. "What's probably best for both of us is for you to see this through. Do what you need to do. And I don't want you to factor me into any decisions you make. That's not really fair to either one of us, and I understand that what's happening with you now was before me."

He starts to say something. I can see that he wants to disagree but realizes that I'm right. Not that I want to be, but I know that I am.

"I'll go back to my room and let you book a flight."

"Dillon, I'm sorry."

"Don't be," I say. "It's been an amazing few days. I won't ever forget them." I start to leave then before he can try to stop me. It wouldn't take much.

"Dillon," he calls out. But I keep walking. I let myself into my room, close the door, and lock it.

~

I HEAD STRAIGHT for the shower, shucking off my

clothes and stepping under the cold spray, hoping it will wash away the memories of this night.

I have no right to cry, but somehow I find myself doing it anyway. Tipping my head against the shower wall, letting the water sluice across my face.

It's not as if I hadn't known all along that we were living a fantasy, that it would have to come to an end eventually. I had known this on some level, and maybe I had just closed it out a little too well.

I have a life to go back to. A life to finish closing up and figuring out. And with the reality of that phone call a few minutes ago, I know that Klein does as well.

I hoped this would go somewhere. I can't deny that deep down, I had imagined what it would be like to continue what we've started when we got back to Nashville. But Klein has a child, a newborn baby, and a connection to his or her mother, whether I want to admit it or not.

He's a good guy, and good guys do the right thing. I know in my heart that he will offer to be there for Riley. If he didn't do that, he wouldn't be the man I know him to be. It's not as if I can even resent this or wish for it to be different.

What we've had here has been a lovely respite from reality. It's the best thing for both of us that the phone call came when it did. There would only have been more to regret, and I'm not going to need that, for sure.

There's only one choice, and that is to let him go. No

strings attached. I don't want him to feel that he owes me anything, because he doesn't. I got from this experience as much as I gave, and that is all that matters.

He texts me a few minutes after I get out of the shower, and says he has booked a flight for seven A.M. out of the Marseille Provence Airport.

I text him back and tell him I'll be glad to drive him, which means we'll have to leave in thirty minutes or so, but I'm not going to sleep anyway. He says he'll be happy to go by car service, but I tell him there's no need, and we leave it at that. I arrange to meet him downstairs in a half-hour, and wonder even as I do if this is the last time I will ever see him again.

Klein

"The pain of parting is nothing to the joy of meeting
again."
—Charles Dickens, *Nicholas Nickleby*

I FEEL AS if someone has inserted a knife in my back, and I'm being ripped apart down the middle.

We're in the car, twenty minutes or so from the airport. We've said very little since leaving the château. Everything has changed between us. I feel it like the shift in barometric pressure before a hurricane. We may not be able to see what is coming, but we both feel it, and there is no escaping it.

I want to reach out and put my hand over hers, but it's clear that I no longer have any right to do that. I want to tell her that somehow, someway, we'll get back to this. But again, I have no idea whether that is true or not, and I know that I cannot lead her along and make her think something might be when I have no idea whether I can give her that.

We're almost to the airport exit when I finally find the words to say what I'm feeling. "Dillon—"

"Yeah," she says, her voice deliberately light.

"I need you to know exactly what being here with you has meant to me."

"Klein, you don't have to—"

"Yes, I do have to. You've made me want things again that I thought I no longer wanted. With my music and my life in general, you've made me see it in a completely different way, and I will forever be grateful to you for that."

"I can say the same thing about you. Maybe we were meant to spend this time together to give each other a new perspective, a new outlook."

I consider my words carefully. "I want it to be about more than that," I say.

"Klein, don't. It can't be, and we both know it."

I start to deny it, but I respect her too much for that. She deserves better.

We're a mile or so from the airport now, and my heart rate kicks up. I feel sick at the thought of leaving.

"The truth is, Klein," she says now, "I have things I have to take care of in my life, too. And I've been kidding myself here, putting it off when I know I can't do that."

"You mean with Josh?"

"Yes," she says. "I mean, he wants us to try again, and I don't know. Maybe I need to give it a shot."

"Is that what you want?" I ask, a little stunned. She won't look at me, and in the near dark of the car I can't read her expression.

"We were married a long time," she says. "Maybe that's not something I should just throw away."

I feel floored by this, wondering if she's just saying it because of what's happened tonight, or if it's something she's really considering. "I thought you were over him," I say.

"He's asked me for another chance," Dillon says softly.

"Oh," I say. "Okay."

We drive the last half mile or so to the departure gates in silence. Dillon pulls the car to the American Airlines entrance, and we sit for a moment, awkward.

A traffic security guard waves for us to move along, and I look at Dillon and say, "This isn't how I wanted this to end."

"I know," she says. "But it's probably for the best, don't you think?"

"When will you be coming back?" I ask.

"I'm not sure," she says. "I may stay at the château another day or two, try to write a few things I have in my head."

"Will you let me know when you're back in Nashville?"

"Sure," she says, and I hear in her voice the unlikelihood that this will actually happen.

I get out of the car, open the back to pull out my suitcase and guitar. I walk around to the driver's door. Dillon has rolled the window down and looks up at me with a forced smile. I feel a deep and immediate grief for what I know has been lost between us, and yet, I don't have the ability or the right to fix it. "Dillon—"

"Don't," she says. "Just go, Klein. Be well and happy, and I'll listen for you on the radio."

I shouldn't because it will only make things worse for both of us, but I lean down and kiss her softly. I feel her give and realize that she's doing what she thinks she needs to do in letting me go. She's doing this for me.

A lump forms in my throat, and I can't seem to swallow past it. My eyes sting with tears. I am not going to let myself lose it in front of her. I step back, pick up my belongings, and walk into the airport.

Dillon

"Maybe all one can do is hope to end up with the right
regrets."
—Arthur Miller

WHEN I GET back to the château, I barely remember
the drive from the airport here. Suddenly I'm parked in the
lot, where we left the car when we first arrived, and the
sun is coming up behind the estate.

I get out of the car, take the path that leads to the
orchard, putting one foot in front of the other without
letting myself think beyond the physical movement.

When I reach the edge of the orchard, I stop for a
minute, staring at the beautiful fruit-laden trees and feeling
the loss of Klein here, as I would a death. I know this
because the hole in my heart is so like the same kind of
grief I had felt after losing my mother, my best friend in
life, someone I knew I could never replace.

I can't deny that this glimpse of happiness I experienced

273

with Klein during our time together in France feels like something I've never found before him, and very likely will never find again.

I walk further into the orchard, sit down on the dew-moist grass, and listen to the morning sounds of the countryside around me. The birds chirp back and forth, busy and happy. I picture Klein and me here, kissing under the warm sun, the smell of ripening fruit abundant all around us. The tears well in my eyes now, slide down my cheeks, and I don't bother to deny them or stop them. I know enough about emotions to know that there is only one way to get past them, and that is to go through them, to feel them.

The sounds of my heartbroken sobbing quiets the birds, as if they respect their interpretation of my language. Once my sorrow is spent, I sit for a while, letting myself absorb this place and its beauty, neither of which I ever want to forget. And when the birds start their singing again, I stand and walk back to the château.

Life does, after all, go on.

~

I STOP FOR a cup of coffee at the front door, the smell drawing me into the enormous foyer. André is standing by the coffee setup and glances at me in surprise.

"Hey," he says. "Good morning. What happened to you two last night?"

"We just decided to head back. It was a lot of fun, though. Thank you so much for inviting us."

"What did you do with Klein this morning? He is not up this early?"

"Actually, I just dropped him off at the airport. He had an emergency back home. He had to leave."

"Oh," André says, looking surprised. "You'll stay with us a bit longer, then?"

"I'm actually not sure yet. This all came up kind of suddenly, and our plans got changed. So I need to figure out what I'm doing."

"Yeah. I understand that," André says. "But if you'd like to get dinner tonight or something, Elizabetta and I would love to do that."

"Thank you," I say. "That's really nice."

"Absolutely," he says. "And if you decide you'd like to go for a ride this afternoon, come to the stables."

"Thank you again," I say, and head toward the elevator with my coffee.

Once I get to the room, I close the door and stare at the furnishings, realizing how empty the place feels now without Klein. Suddenly, I can't imagine staying here without him. And I don't want to.

Riley

"I have formed my plans—right plans I deem them. . ."
—Charlotte Brontë, *Jane Eyre*

THINGS HAVE NOT worked out as I imagined they would.

The baby is two months early, and I am filled with an unreasonable terror that I will be left with no cards to play. Even in my current state of agony, I realize how callous and cold this sounds, but I'm nothing if not realistic. Without this baby, there is no chance of me ever having Klein.

Dagger-sharp pain stabs through the middle of my body, and it is all I can do not to lunge from the bed and grab the sympathetic-looking nurse standing beside the IV pole and shake her until she adds something to the plastic bag cocktail that will take away this agony.

Through clenched teeth, I manage to say, "When will the doctor be here?"

"As soon as you are dilated a little more, he will come in to check you."

"And the epidural?" I almost scream.

"I'm so sorry, my dear. It's way too late for that."

"What? What do you mean, 'It's way too late'?"

"You're too far along," the nurse says, and some part of me wonders if she's taking a little too much pleasure in this announcement. Her sympathy seems to have faded and been replaced with an awareness of how close I am to strangling her. If I thought I could get away with it, I'm pretty sure I would, simply as a release for my own despair.

"I'm afraid there's no possibility of rowing backward from here, my dear. You've got to row upstream now," she says in her cheerful nurse voice.

I now know for sure if I had the means to do so, I would gladly strangle her. But another slice of pain sears through me, and it is all I can do not to scream, grappling for self-control.

I have always prided myself on being able to suffer through what others could not seem to. When I was twelve, I was having a tooth filled when the novocain wore off. I forced myself not to tell the dentist because I wanted to see if I could actually bear it, and I did.

But this was something altogether different. The pain feels as if it starts at the top of my head, boring through me with the ferocity of a lightning bolt slamming through an oak tree.

It's then that I realize I'm not afraid for the baby's life; I'm afraid for my own.

Klein

"If you tell the truth, you don't have to remember
anything."
—Mark Twain

MY FLIGHT TO Nashville goes through Atlanta, and
by the time we touch down, it is a full eighteen hours since
I received the call from Curtis. I had grappled with the
thought of texting Riley, but I'm afraid to give her a heads-
up. I don't want her to know that I know anything. Given
the fact that she lied to me, I have no idea what to expect
when she finds out I know.

I get an Uber from the airport and go straight to
Vanderbilt. My suitcase and guitar are still with me. The
Uber driver lets me out at the hospital's front entrance. I
walk up to the information desk, the woman working
behind it looking up. "I'm wondering if you would mind
holding my guitar and suitcase here while I go upstairs and

visit someone. And if you promise not to let on that I'm in the hospital, I'll give you two front-row tickets to my next concert."

She smiles at me and says, "Oh, you don't have to do that. Your secret's good with me, Mr. Matthews. I'm a big fan, and I'm happy to do that for you."

I take note of her name tag so I can send something for her later, and give her a sincere, "Thank you," before heading for the elevators.

Curtis had texted just before I landed and given me Riley's room number. I press the button for the floor and push back a weight of nervousness. He hadn't been able to tell me anything other than Riley was still in the hospital. He had no news of the baby.

The elevator doors open, and I step out into the hallway, looking left then right and following the numbers on the wall to Riley's room. The door is cracked, and I stick my head around the edge before knocking.

She is asleep. There's no one else in the room, so I step quietly inside. I walk over to the bed and stand there, looking down at her. She looks peaceful and exhausted, even in sleep.

I wonder how things could have gone so wrong between us, how we've arrived at a place where we've failed each other so miserably.

Riley opens her eyes wide as if she has heard my

thoughts. She stares at me for a couple of seconds before saying, "Klein? What are you doing here?"

"Curtis called me and said that you were in the hospital having a baby."

Her eyes go wider, and she has the look of someone who's been caught in an awful lie. Which she has.

"Did you have the baby, Riley?" I'm holding my breath for her answer, part of me desperate to know and another part terrified of the answer. That something will have gone wrong.

Shock is replaced with something much more like anger, and she says, "Yes. But I owe you nothing, Klein, much less an explanation."

"Yes, you do owe me an explanation, Riley. You told me you'd—"

"Because you didn't want me," she interrupts, trying to sit up in bed, and suddenly I feel guilty for upsetting her when she's obviously worn out.

"I don't want to know anything right now except whether the baby is okay or not."

I watch as she wrestles with an answer. I'm guessing she knows there's no point in lying since all I have to do is walk outside and find the nurse to discover the answer for myself.

She relents, then reluctantly says, "She's early and in the neonatal unit. I was so out of it when the doctor was explaining things to me that I'm not sure what's going to happen."

She. A baby girl. Emotion grips my heart. "Are you okay?" I ask.

"Yes. I think so," she says, looking surprised that I've asked.

"I'm going to go check on her. I'll come back and let you know what I find out, okay?"

"Yes," she says, more contrite now than I've ever seen her. She lies back on the pillow, closing her eyes.

Rather than ask which floor the neonatal care unit is on, I pull my phone from my pocket and do a quick search. Turns out, it's on the same floor, so I follow the signs until I find it.

Approaching a nearby nurse station, I find that I have no idea how to explain my situation. So I decide to go for the closest version of the truth I can manage. I tell her that my ex-girlfriend has delivered our premature baby, and I would very much like to see her.

The nurse I've approached is older, with steel-gray hair tucked into a bun at the nape of her neck. Her expression says she has pretty much seen and heard it all.

And so for once, I decide to use the fact that she might recognize me. I take off my cap, and it's only a couple of seconds before recognition flashes in her eyes, and she says, "Oh, my! You're Klein Matthews."

"Sorry, I just wanted you to know I'm not some psycho

coming in off the street trying to look at someone else's baby."

"Does the mother know you're here?"

"She does. I just left her room."

"Okay. Follow me, Mr. Matthews."

I do, down the hall to a set of doors, which she leads me through with a renewed sense of purpose.

The neonatal intensive care unit is behind a long stretch of windows through which I can see several babies in their tiny incubators being watched over by very attentive nurses.

My heart pumps wildly against my chest as I scan the tiny faces in search of the little girl I instinctively know I will recognize. And I do well before the nurse who has brought me here manages to get the attention of one of the caretakers inside the unit.

"That's her," I say, pointing to the tiny baby in the far right corner of the room. The nurse's gaze goes to the baby I've pointed out. I hear her sigh of sympathy, and I swallow hard to prevent the sob in my throat from slipping out.

"The nurses and doctors who oversee these babies are just absolutely the best," she reassures me. "I know your little one is here way early, but you would be amazed how successful they are at helping these tiny angels thrive and grow. Your little girl is going to be just fine," the nurse says, grazing my arm with her soft hand.

I glance at her, unable to hide my anguish now, and say,

"Thank you. I am so grateful to hear that. Is there any way I could go in?"

"I'm afraid not right now," she says with sympathy. "As soon as the doctor says it's okay, we'll get you in there and scrubbed up so that you can see her."

"Thank you," I say, genuinely appreciative of her kindness. "Would it be all right if I just stand out here and watch her for a while?"

"Of course," she says. "You stay as long as you'd like. I'm going to head back to my station now."

"Thank you," I say again. She pats me on the shoulder and sets off down the hall, her rubber soles squeaking on the floor.

I turn back to the glass window and stare at the tiny baby I am half-responsible for bringing into this world. I realize I don't even know her name or if she has one yet.

I fix my gaze on her small face and wish more than anything that I could pick her up and hold her just so she could know how much she's loved and how much she's wanted. Because the moment I knew of her existence, I loved her. I grieved for her when I thought she would never live in this world. It feels like a miracle to see her here. Even with her fragile grasp on life, it is a miracle. I do realize that. I drop my head, close my eyes, and begin to pray a prayer of thanks.

Dillon

"I know my heart will never be the same
But I'm telling myself I'll be okay"
—Sara Evans, "A Little Bit Stronger"

I DECIDE TO drive the car back to Paris and leave from there. I spend nearly a full day driving, taking my time on the unfamiliar roads. I stay in a hotel near the airport, and my flight is early.

I want to text Klein and ask him how the baby is, but I refuse to let myself. This will go better for both of us if we don't open the door again, and me asking questions of any kind would be doing exactly that.

On the plane, I pull out my laptop, pop in my headphones, and consider working on some new lyrics. But I find myself tapping my recording app and clicking on the song Klein and I had written.

I lean back and close my eyes, letting the words and

his beautiful voice wash over me. Tears rise up. I blink them back, knowing I should turn the song off. But I'm a glutton for punishment, and as soon as he finishes, I click play and start it over again.

Josh

"Opportunities are like sunrises. If you wait too long, you
miss them."
—**William Arthur Ward**

I DON'T KNOW what makes me decide to text Dillon
to check in when I do, but I end up being glad that I did.
She answers me right away, surprisingly, and says that she's
on a flight headed for Nashville and will be landing in two
hours.

I offer to pick her up at the airport and, again to my
surprise, she accepts. I'm waiting on the other side of
security when she comes into sight. For a moment, I'm
overcome with the need to make up for my wrongs. She
approaches me with a polite smile, as if we are more
colleagues or acquaintances than husband and wife.

"Hey," I say, when she comes to a stop in front of me.

"Hi, Josh. How are you?"

287

"I'm all right," I say. "You look great."

"That's a surprise considering the flight. I feel pretty rumpled."

"No, really you do," I say, and I mean that. She looks five years younger. Is that what Paris does for you? Or was it something else? Jealousy stabs my heart as I say, "Here, let me take your bag."

I reach for the small pull-behind, and we walk toward the exit, awkward and quiet until she breaks the silence with, "Everything going all right with the business?"

"Yeah," I say. "Actually, really good. Signed a new female artist who's killing it."

"That's great," she says, and there's something in her voice that makes me wonder if she's really interested.

We've reached the car and are both sitting inside when she says, "About Klein. Just so you know, I'm not pursuing that. It was petty of me, I guess. I was looking for some way to get back at you and that seemed like something that definitely would."

I sit for a moment with my hands on the steering wheel and finally find the voice to say, "I deserve pretty much anything you can think of in the way of retaliation, Dillon. I'm not going to deny that. I treated you horribly, and no apology is ever going to make up for that. All I can ask is that somehow, someway could you please, please find it in your heart to give me another chance? I swear I'll make it up to you."

She lets out a small sigh and leans her head against the back of the seat. "It's a big ask, Josh."

"I know," I say.

I stay quiet this time, knowing she's right and what I've broken certainly qualifies for unfixable status. "Can we just go home and take a bit to think about things? I'll sleep in the guest room. It would be nice to have you there, Dillon, and there's no reason for you to be in a hotel or—" I stop then and add, "If you would like for me to leave the house, I will do that. You can be there."

She closes her eyes and sighs again. "I'm really tired, Josh. For tonight, it's fine for us both to be there. We'll figure it out in the morning."

"Okay," I say, and although she has given me no hope whatsoever, somehow I feel that this is at least a positive sign.

Dillon

"Stronger than lover's love is lover's hate. Incurable, in
each, the wounds they make."
—**Euripides**

IT TAKES ME hours to go to sleep that night. Maybe
it's because I feel like I'm in a stranger's house, but actually,
it's the bedroom I've shared with Josh for years. I no longer
feel as if I belong here. The bed is strange and foreign, a
reminder of a time in our marriage I would now rather
forget. As for the good times, I try to imagine it being that
way, and I can't. I just can't. Some part of me knows that
this stage of my life is truly over. I know Josh wants me
to say something different, but we shared a mostly silent
dinner at the kitchen table earlier. The food tasted like
sawdust in my mouth. The bottle of wine he had opened
only enhanced my reservations about being here.

I had realized one thing, though, sitting across from
him and seeing for myself that he really does mean it this

time when he says he wants another chance. I realize that I'm no longer angry with him. I left that somewhere in France. I'm not sure at what point it dissipated into indifference, but the fire that had propelled me across the ocean to Paris on a mission of vengeance has petered out, and, in its place, there is only a sense of peace now. I can picture nothing of my future except this one thing. I know that Josh and I will not be together.

~

WHEN I WAKE up the next morning, it's almost ten. I raise up on one elbow and stare at the alarm clock on the nightstand, trying to bring the numbers into focus, realizing I slept far later than I intended to. I turn over. The sound of paper rumples beneath me. It's a note from Josh.

Good morning. Sorry to leave so early, but I have a meeting. You know where the coffee is, and I'll call you in a bit. Josh.

I lie back again, staring at the ceiling and wondering if I am being hardhearted. Josh is trying. There's no doubt about that. There's something I know this morning that I may not have known yesterday. I can't spend the rest of my life with Josh, but I do forgive him, and there's peace in that for me, and I hope there will be for him as well.

~

WHEN MY CELL phone rings, I don't recognize the

number on the screen. I consider ignoring it, imagining it will be yet another of those robotic sales calls that aggravate me to the point that I hang up even as I feel guilty for the bad manners. So I'm not sure why but I tap the screen and answer with a brisk, "Hello?"

"Dillon."

"Yes?" I say, not recognizing the voice.

"This is Riley Haverson."

To say I'm surprised would be an understatement of epic proportions. I have no idea why she would be calling me, but I say, "Yes. Riley. What can I do for you?"

"A number of things, actually," she says, her voice laced with confidence. "I was wondering if you would mind visiting me at the hospital. I'm at Vanderbilt."

My surprise has now turned to shock. "I'm not sure that's really a good idea."

"It's an excellent idea, all things considered."

"Are you okay?" I ask, realizing we'd skipped all the preliminaries of admitting that to this point, we've never even spoken to each other before.

"I'm doing well, yes, but there is something I would like to discuss with you. Can you come this morning?"

Every instinct inside me screams that the answer should be no, or that I should at least check with Klein first, but something else, maybe something as basic as curiosity, has me saying, "Yes. What time?"

"An hour or so would be great," she says, and gives me

the room number. "Thank you, Dillon," she adds, and hangs up.

I sit for a moment staring at the phone screen, sure that I should call Klein's number and tell him about this request. But I don't. It's a short drive from the house I've lived in with Josh to the hospital. With traffic, it takes me less than fifteen minutes. I park my car in the hospital garage, take the elevator to the lobby, and then another elevator to the floor where Riley's room is. My stomach has become a knot of nerves, and a wave of nausea has me stopping by a restroom and splashing cold water on my face. I grab a paper towel, dab away the water and stare at my pale complexion in the mirror.

This is crazy. It makes no sense at all. So why am I doing it? I have no answer for the question except to leave the restroom and walk the short corridor to Riley's room number. I stop at the partially closed door, take a deep breath, and rap once.

"Come in."

I push the door open and step into the room. I'm not sure what I expected, but it isn't to see Riley in bed looking as if she just stepped out of a salon. She is undeniably beautiful with thick, shoulder-length blonde hair and long-lashed blue eyes. I feel instantly frumpy.

"Thank you for coming, Dillon," Riley says. "Please, sit down."

I take the chair near the bed, and say, "I'm glad to see that you're okay. And the baby?"

"Our baby is fine," she says. "Klein's and mine."

I give this a pause, pretty sure I know where we're going. "If you asked me here to make sure that I'm aware of what's between you and Klein, there was no need to do that. I have no holds on Klein."

"That's very nice to hear," Riley says. "After I became aware of the two of you meeting up in Paris and saw the photo of you, I thought it might be something other than friendship."

I start to deny it but realize I'm not going to lie to her. Klein and I aren't anything now, but what we might've become, I don't know. And so I simply wait for her to speak.

"Look, Dillon. I know this is awkward, but Klein and I have pretty significant history, and now we have a child together."

I try to stop myself. I know I should, but the words are out before I can stop them. "So why did you lie to him?"

My question takes her by surprise. I'm not sure if it's because she thinks Klein would not have told me this, or that I have the gumption to ask her. Either way, a spurt of anger flashes through her eyes, and she says, "Is that really any of your business?"

"I consider Klein a friend and a truly good man. Yeah, I kind of think it is."

She gives me a long considering look, as if she's trying to weigh the likelihood of my being an actual adversary. When she finally replies, her voice is deliberately low and even. "I was hoping once you knew about the baby, you would understand anything that might have happened between Klein and me before this as being just the kind of thing people go through when they're trying to figure out whether they belong together or not. I wasn't sure that Klein wanted to be with me because he loved me or if it would only be because of the baby. I guess I thought that mattered, but what I realize now is the only thing that really matters is that Noelle has two parents who truly love her."

"And you do," I ask, "love her?"

The anger that flashes across Riley's face now is something altogether different from the smoldering embers she let me see a few moments ago. This one is involuntary, as if it has risen up from some bottomless volcano pit, outrage at its flaming tip. "I think you are deceiving me, Dillon. I think that you want Klein for yourself, and you're jealous of what he and I now have. Something I understand you probably can't give him."

The jab takes its intended aim, stabbing me in the heart as only truth can. "How do you know that?"

"Rumors in Nashville are usually fairly reliable. I can see that they weren't wrong this time. I'm sorry that you've had cancer. That isn't something I would wish on anyone.

295

However, we all have our crosses to bear in this life. I've certainly had mine, not the same as yours, I'm sure, but mine all the same. Poverty is something I never intend to live again, and Klein and I will be able to give this little angel everything her heart desires."

I listen to the words as something awful settles over me. A question that comes out of nowhere. What exactly would Riley do to keep him? I know she lied about not keeping the baby. What else?

"Does Klein feel the same?" I ask.

"What do you mean?"

"Does he intend to raise Noelle as you've just said?"

"Klein will do whatever I want him to, and of course, he's already madly in love with her. Why wouldn't he give her whatever she wants or needs?"

"I have no doubt of Klein's love for her, but sometimes love is about more than possessions."

"That's easy to say when you've had all of that," Riley snaps back, "as I'm sure you no doubt have, Dillon. You, being songwriter of the year married to Josh Cummings. I'm sorry that you couldn't hold on to your husband, keep him out of another woman's bed, but that doesn't mean that you should resort to stealing another woman's man."

I stand then, realizing it is far past time for me to go. "I think enough has been said, Riley," I say. "Good luck to you." I turn then to leave the room, but she stops me with a venomous hiss.

"Do not underestimate me, Dillon. When I say that I will have him at any cost, that is exactly what I mean."

I turn then, taking in the look of pure hatred on her face. "Is there something you would like to elaborate on, Riley?"

She struggles with the answer, the desire to unleash on me versus the struggle to maintain her composure. "Just know this. I am completely capable of making sure no one else has him."

A chill of disgust ripples across me then, and without giving myself another moment to take in her poisonous words, I open the door and leave the room.

Klein

"An entire sea of water can't sink a ship unless it gets inside the ship. Similarly, the negativity of the world can't put you down unless you allow it to get inside you."

—Goi Nasu

I'M GETTING DRESSED to go to the hospital when the nausea hits me. It is so sudden and with such force that I drop to my knees on the bathroom floor. Within seconds, I am throwing up the orange juice I'd taken my supplements with before getting in the shower. It doesn't let up for a good ten minutes, until there is absolutely nothing left inside me to throw up other than my own insides. I am so spent by the violence of the sickness that I stretch out, face down, on the bathroom's marble floor, closing my eyes and praying that it doesn't hit again.

Finally, convinced that it's over, I roll onto my back and stare at the ceiling, trying to figure out what is going on. This episode is exactly the same as the one I had in

Paris, only worse. My head is starting to pound now, and I feel the intensity of it building. I wonder if I have some horrible disease that I'm only just figuring out. Why would this happen twice with no apparent reason?

I remember the pain medication the doctor in France had given me. I manage to pull myself up to the bathroom counter and find it still inside my shave case. I open the bottle, swallow two tablets with as little water as I can manage and then make my way into the bedroom where I collapse onto the bed.

~

I HAVE NO idea how much time has passed. When I wake up I am groggy and feel as if I've been asleep for a week. I lift up on one elbow, look at the clock and see that it is one in the afternoon. I wait for a moment to see if the headache is gone, and it is. My stomach feels as if it has been rinsed with acid. It aches almost unbearably.

By this point, I'm pretty sure I need to see a doctor. I pick up my cell phone and call my manager.

Curtis answers on the first ring. "Hey," he says.

"I'm a little under the weather. I was wondering if you could get me in with a doctor today?"

"Sure. What's going on, Klein?" he asks with worry in his voice.

"I don't really know. It's the same thing that happened in Paris. I just became uncontrollably sick with a massive headache afterward. It's happened again this morning, so I have no idea, but I don't think it's anything good."

"Yeah, man," Curtis says. "I know a guy over at Vanderbilt. Let me give him a ring and see what I can get going. I'll be back in touch with you in just a bit, okay?"

"Thank you," I say and hang up.

It's less than five minutes before Curtis calls back. "I'm going to come over and pick you up. The appointment is in an hour with Dr. Macau. He was happy to work you in."

"I really appreciate that, Curtis. I was headed to the hospital this morning. My phone is blowing up with texts from Riley. Would you mind calling her? Tell her what's happened and check in on the baby for me, please? I don't think I can right now."

"Of course," Curtis says. "I'll be there in about thirty minutes."

"Yeah. See you then."

~

CURTIS IS TRUE to his word, knocking on my door in exactly a half hour. I've managed to get dressed but am so weak that I can barely walk to the car without his hand at my arm.

"You've got me worried, Klein," Curtis says as he pulls out onto the street from my house. "No idea what's going on?"

"None," I say shaking my head.

"Look, everything's going to be all right. Dr. Macau is the best of the best, and whoever you need to see from there, he'll make excellent recommendations."

"Did you get in touch with Riley? "I ask, leaning my head against the back of the seat and closing my eyes.

"I did," Curtis says. "Can't say she was any too happy until I told her you were sick. Then she put on her compassionate hat. I'm sorry. I shouldn't have said that. I know she's the mother of your child, but good lord, Klein."

"Yeah, I know," I say.

~

DR. MACAU IS as good as Curtis promised he would be. In his office at Vanderbilt, he asks me dozens of questions before ever taking a look at me. Among them, questions about where I've been recently, what I've eaten, had to drink, things I might've been exposed to, people I've been with. I begin to wonder where he's going with this, but he's doesn't give me any clues.

Once he's completed the questions, he calls a nurse, a kind, motherly older woman, who greets me with a reassuring smile and asks me to please follow her. I do so and end up in an examination room where she tells me to put on a lovely blue paper gown and lets me know that the doctor will be in very soon. He is and gives me the most thorough examination I've ever had in my life. Once that's complete, he says, "Klein, I'd like to get some blood work, get a urine sample, and if you don't mind, I'd like to take a sample of your hair from the back of your head. It won't be noticeable. We'll get it so that you'll never even know it was done."

Of everything he's said, I find this the most alarming, not out of vanity, but concern for what the reason would be. "I have to ask you, doctor, what are you thinking?"

"Just trying to cover all the bases, Klein, and since you were in another country and your activities have been a little unusual, I'd like to make sure you haven't taken in some kind of toxic substance. We'll do a tox screen."

This, of all things, is not what I expected to hear. "What kind of toxin?"

"It could be anything," Dr. Macau says, shaking his head a little. "But your symptoms are fairly unusual given that there doesn't seem to be any prompting factor."

"Yeah," I say. "Okay. Whatever you need to do."

Once I'm done, I walk back to the waiting room where Curtis is looking at a magazine and waiting for me.

"Everything go okay?"

"Yeah, yeah," I say. "I'm not sure what to make of it, but I guess we'll find out what he thinks at some point."

"It's probably nothing," Curtis says. "A virus or some bug you picked up. Better to cover all the bases though, right?"

I agree with a silent nod and we walk from the office to the parking lot, getting back in Curtis's car.

"He did do some kind of weird testing, though, and when I asked him why, he indicated he wanted to make sure I hadn't taken in anything toxic."

"You mean like you were poisoned?" Curtis asked.

"I really don't know," I say. "I mean accidentally of course. I didn't deliberately expose myself to anything."

"Right," Curtis says, but he looks a little startled by the revelation, and if I didn't feel so weak and out of it, I would ask him why. I don't have the strength for the conversation right now, so I just close my eyes and let him drive me home.

Riley

"Some allies are more dangerous than enemies."
—George R.R. Martin

I AM MORE than ready to be released from the hospital. My stay has been longer than the average delivery stay because I seem to have developed an infection that the doctors want to make sure isn't going to be an issue before they release me. I'm beyond bummed that Klein hasn't shown up today and not sure what to make of Curtis's explanation. He'd said Klein was unable to come because he had been sick this morning. I'm beginning to regret my rash decision to pay Klein back with a few bouts of violent illness.

I mean, what if it actually kills him? Then what would I do? We're not married. No provisions have been made for the baby since Klein hadn't even known about her. A hard wedge of fury forces its way up from somewhere deep inside me, and I curse my ignorance. I may end up being my own worst enemy, after all.

A rap at the door interrupts my worrying. "Come in," I say, hopeful that Klein has recovered enough to make it here today. But the face that appears is not one I had expected. "Pete," I say, not bothering to hide my irritation. "What are you doing here?"

His boots thud heavily on the hospital floor. "I just came by to check in and see how you're doing."

"There's absolutely no reason on earth why that would be necessary or expected."

"I'm sure of that," he says, walking around the bed to take a seat in the chair next to me. I'm glad suddenly that Noelle can't stay in the room yet. I don't want him to tarnish the promise of her birth with memories of the payment I'd had to make for Pete's silence.

"Why are you here, Pete?" I ask, trying not to make the words an actual hiss.

"That's an understandable question on your part. I got a call from Curtis a little while ago. It seems that he took Klein to see a doctor this morning."

"Yes, I know he's not feeling well," I say, keeping my voice neutral.

Pete looks at me for a long, hard moment, and a chill creeps its way down my spine.

"I'm a little curious about something Curtis said."

"Oh, really? What would that be?"

"He said the doctor wondered if Klein might've been exposed to something toxic." He drops the last words like a quarter in a slot machine, my response his potential prize.

"That would be odd, wouldn't it?" I say in as clipped a tone as I can manage.

"It would," Pete agrees. "And not something I would ordinarily think anything about except that there is this thing I found out about you and Aaron, which I know I never actually completely conveyed to you. There really didn't seem to be any point in going over that when we had agreed on a deal for my silence. But now I'm wondering if maybe that had been a rash decision on my part."

"What exactly do you think you know, Pete?"

"I know that one day when Aaron and I were hanging out having a beer, and he was talking to me about his depression, he confided that you had actually suggested he might want to commit suicide."

The words drop across me like bullets at a target, punching holes as they land. "If you knew him, surely you know that Aaron tended to exaggerate."

"Actually," Pete says, "I knew him to be an extremely kind soul who never hurt anyone in his life. I also know that he was madly in love with you, or at least he thought he was, but he did struggle with depression, like many creative people I know. He seemed to think that once you figured out he probably wasn't going to get to the rung on the ladder of life you were aiming for, you were pretty much done with him."

"That is insane," I say. "And that might be an accurate word to describe Aaron in the last year of his life."

"You see," Pete says, giving me a long cold stare. "I have to disagree with that because I knew him well. I spent a lot of time with Aaron in the last year of his life. That's not what I saw at all. I saw a man with a broken heart for sure and a man struggling with clinical depression."

"And he told you that I said he should kill himself? I don't know. Maybe I did say that in the heat of one of our arguments or something, but who doesn't say things like that now and then?"

He considers this for several loud seconds. "I can't say that I know anyone who does. You see, I saw the texts that you sent him, not just one but several. And they all said exactly that, that when a person gets as sad as he was, maybe there really is no other option for ending it."

I consider my response for some time. I could deny it, but he said he saw the texts, so that would be pointless. I opt for another strategy. "And do you think you're so much better than me, Pete? You who angled to sleep with me using this very information? How do you figure that makes you any better than me at all?"

"It doesn't," Pete says. "I readily admit it. I've never claimed to be any kind of saint, far from it, in fact. And if I had it to do over again, I probably would pass on that little piece of blackmail I pulled with you. But there you go. We don't get to redo many of our mistakes in this life, do we? However, when I was talking to Curtis this morning, and he mentioned the whole poisoning thing, I wondered what lengths you might go to when Klein made it clear he didn't want a future with you? Am I getting close, Riley?"

I feel the blood leave my face. I'm really a better liar than this, but somehow he's caught me off guard, and I am all but handing him a winning ticket.

"You have no idea what you're talking about, Pete," I say. But even to my ears, the words are unconvincing.

He shrugs. "Maybe not, but I've lost one buddy to you, Riley. And even though I would never call myself a great friend to Klein, I'm not so far down the road that I would let him get thrown under the bus by you, too."

"Get out, Pete," I say, my teeth literally clenched together. I want to pick up the closest object and hurl it at him, but that would only bring a barrage of nurses running, and right now, I just need to be by myself to regroup, to think.

"You take care now, Riley," he says, getting up and stopping at the doorway. He turns around to look at me one more time. But it's not gloating that I see there. It's something that looks a lot more like regret.

Klein

"Yet each man kills the thing he loves
By each let this be heard
Some do it with a bitter look
Some with a flattering word
The coward does it with a kiss
The brave man with a sword"
—Oscar **Wilde**

I AM JUST ABOUT ready to leave the house for the hospital when a knock sounds at the front door. I'm not expecting anyone, so I look out the window. Curtis's car sits in the circular drive. I open the door, figuring he's stopped by just to check in on me. "Hey," I say.

"How are you?" he asks, walking into the foyer.

"Feeling a lot better."

"Glad to hear it," he says with a weary sigh. "We need to talk, Klein."

I hear the concern in his voice and wonder if the doctor

might have gotten back to him, but then doctors don't do that. They communicate directly with their patient. "Come in, Curtis."

He walks through the foyer and into the living room, coming to a stop in front of the fireplace. His hands are shoved inside his pockets, a look of unease on his face.

"I can tell something is wrong, Curtis. Just go ahead and say it."

"I hate to be the bearer of this kind of news, but there's no way to get around it. You have to know about this, and then you can figure out what to make of it or what to do about it."

"What is it?" I say, feeling an awful sense of dread.

"Pete stopped by to see me a little while ago. He'd been to the hospital to see Riley and apparently had an enlightening conversation with her."

"About what?" I ask, deadpan.

"He knew the guy Riley dated before you, Aaron Rutgers. I think you probably met him a few times."

"Yeah," I say.

"He seems to think Riley played a part in Aaron's suicide."

This is the last thing I expect to hear. Shock reverberates through me. "What do you mean, 'played a part'?"

"He says he saw texts from her telling Aaron he should kill himself."

"What? Wait a minute, Curtis. There are a lot of things

about Riley that wouldn't surprise me, but that she would do something like that, I can't imagine."

"Neither can I, but maybe you should talk to Pete. It's pretty convincing. He said he actually read the text. It wasn't just hearsay."

I have no idea what to say. It's as if a bomb has gone off inside me, and all of a sudden, I'm thinking that Riley, a woman who might do something as cruel as this, is the mother of the baby I already can't imagine living without. "So, why are you telling me this now?"

"Because that's not all there is to it, Klein."

"What else could there be?"

Curtis drops his head back a couple of inches, staring up at the ceiling as if looking for inspiration and then says, "Pete thinks she might be behind whatever has been making you sick."

If the information about Aaron had been a shock, I have no words to describe the effect this bombshell has on me. "That's just crazy."

"I know it is," Curtis admits, shrugging a little. "She hasn't even been around you, has she?"

"No. Not for a good while."

"Then maybe Pete's just overthinking it."

But then I remember the text from Riley when I'd been in Paris, a reminder to take my vitamins. Could she have put something in them? I can't imagine. But.

"I'm sorry, Klein. Whatever I can do," Curtis says,

slapping a reassuring hand on my shoulder. "You know I'll do it."

"I do," I say. Curtis lets himself out of the house with a bit of a dip to his shoulders. He's a bright, sunshiny kind of guy, and I know this kind of thing upsets the natural goodness he likes to afford people. I'd like to believe there's nothing about this that could possibly be true, but something in my gut knows it is. There's only one way I'm going to find out, and that's to talk to Riley in person.

~

I DON'T TELL her what time I'm coming, but nonetheless, when I walk into Riley's room, she's alone, and I'm glad because I can't hold in my questions much longer.

"Hey," she says. "I'm so glad you're here. They're saying I can probably go home today."

"That's good," I say in an even voice, walking over to stand by the window and stare down at the parking lot below. "We need to talk, Riley," I say without looking at her yet. For some reason, I can't bring myself to do so, and I fold my arms across my chest, getting to the point immediately. "Pete thinks you might be trying to get rid of me, Riley."

As soon as the words leave my mouth, I do turn to look at her, wanting to gauge her reaction for myself. I can see she's been expecting this because her expression is completely neutral. There's not a glimpse of surprise to an eyebrow nor a shocked widening of her eyes.

"Pete's crazy," she says.

"You can have your opinion about that, nonetheless, he's pretty convinced of what he's saying."

She shakes her head and rolls her eyes. "Why on earth would I do something like that, Klein?"

"I don't know, Riley. Why would you? Maybe to pay me back. All I know is I've been sick twice and have no explanation for it. My doctor was a little curious, so he insisted on doing a tox screen. Is there anything in there that you think he might find?"

Riley's face blanches an unnatural shade of white. I watch as she silently grapples for an answer, and I really don't need to hear anything more from her. It's clear that there's enough truth to this accusation to make me sure I want to see the results of Dr. Macau's testing. And get him to test the rest of my supplements as well.

Dillon

"How often have I lain beneath rain on a strange roof,
thinking of home."
—**William C. Faulkner**

I HONESTLY THINK I'd forgotten how much I love
it here.

Mama left me the house on Smith Mountain Lake. The
Virginia land and old farmhouse were left to her by her
parents. I've only been here once since she died, and
pulling into the driveway now, I'm overcome with a wave
of sadness. I turn the car off and sit staring at the house,
memories welling up. I see Mama standing on the front
porch, waving at me as I climb on the school bus. I see
our Lab Lucy bounding down the steps to meet me in the
afternoon.

It's summertime here, and I remember countless days
when Mama and I had sat on the front porch on a day

such as this, eating watermelon and having a seed-spitting contest.

Maybe it wasn't a good idea to come now. But honestly, I couldn't think of anywhere else I belong. Nashville felt like a place I needed to leave. The house Josh and I shared wasn't ours anymore. It is his. I wish more than anything in the world that Mama was here to meet me. That I could run up the stairs and into the house to find her in the kitchen baking sugar cookies because she knew I was coming.

But I know she won't be there, and so I get out of the car, walking up the steps and finding the key under the flowerpot by the front door. It fits in the lock exactly the same as the last time I'd used it, just slightly crooked, but the lock cooperates, and the door swings in.

The house always smells the same as I remember, a touch of lemon furniture polish mixed with the scent of yesterday's baking. It's not logical that the house would smell of Mama's cooking, and sometimes, I wonder if it is my memory guiding my senses and not the actual house.

I step inside the foyer, my shoes squeaking on the polished hardwood floor. I've been paying Betsy Harker to clean every two weeks, and looking around, I can see she has kept things exactly as Mama would have. Mama loved a clean house, and she spent every Saturday morning making ours shine. She enlisted my help when I was older, and I never minded because her love for this place had been infused in my heart the same as it had hers.

I flick on lamps as I head toward the kitchen, stopping in the doorway to take in the room Mama had loved most. She'd kept much of it as it had been when she was growing up, the white stove with its gas burners, the farm table in the breakfast nook, the large cupboard with her grandma's dishes prominently displayed.

I stand at the screen door that looks out onto the back yard, note that Betsy's husband is as careful and meticulous with his mowing as she is with cleaning. It's nice to come home and see the place so well taken care of. I know that would make Mama happy.

Why haven't I come home more? I could blame it on Josh and the fact that he'd never been overly enthusiastic about coming here, but the fault is more mine, if I'm honest. I cared what he wanted more than I cared about coming home. I feel heartsick at the pain I must have caused Mama. And now it's too late to undo any of it. Too late to tell her I'm sorry.

I turn and walk back to the truck where I pull my big suitcase from the passenger seat. I'd left the Porsche 911 with Josh. I don't want it anymore. It was never me anyway. I pat the hood of the truck as I roll the suitcase toward the front porch. The truck has always been more me.

~

I TAKE A long hot soak in the bathtub upstairs. It's the old clawfoot kind, and I'm a little tall for it, but it's deep, and the water is deliciously warm, the bubbles I've added floating up under my chin. I close my eyes and try not to think about the scene with Josh before I'd left. I've hurt him. I know it, but it wasn't because I wanted revenge. I just know it's time to move on, figure out where I'm going from here.

My phone rings from the stool near the tub. I sit up and reach for it, glancing at the screen. My heart thuds and takes off at a gallop. Should I answer? Would it be better to leave the connection between us severed?

Probably, but I click the green button anyway. "Hey."

"Dillon. Hey."

His voice drenches me in warmth. I sit up in the bath, pulling my knees against my chest and putting him on speaker. "How are you?" I ask, my voice echoing in the room.

"I'm not too sure," he says, and I can hear that something is terribly wrong. "What's happened, Klein? Is it the baby?"

"No," he says. "She's actually good. Small but the doctors say she's headed in all the right directions. I'm grateful beyond words."

"That's wonderful. I'm so glad." I wait, feeling there's more he wants to say.

"Do you have a minute to talk?"

"Of course."

317

"Something has happened that I'm not sure what to do about."

I hear the weight in his voice and feel a pang of alarm. "What is it, Klein? What's happened?"

"I got sick again the morning after I got back from Paris. The same as that morning at the hotel. I went to see a doctor at Vanderbilt. He ran a tox screen that showed traces of ipecac. It's a substance used to make people throw up if they've ingested poison. The sickness hit me after taking my vitamins in the morning."

"Riley put the ipecac in the capsules." I say this with utter conviction, thinking back to the moments before I left Riley's hospital room, the venom in her voice when she made it clear that if she couldn't have Klein, no one would.

"That's what it looks like."

"Oh, Klein," I say, newly struck with horror for what I am hearing. "Are you okay?"

"Yeah. Fortunately. Apparently, the amount I took in this last time was enough to make me sick but nothing worse. The capsules in some of the pills I hadn't taken yet contained enough to cause a lot more than just vomiting."

"I'm so sorry, Klein. What are you going to do?"

He's quiet for several seconds. And then, "Curtis thinks I need to go the police."

"What do you think?"

"Logically, I know that's the right thing."

"But she's the mother of your child."

His silence tells me I'm right. "I feel sorry for the baby. I mean what a start. First, Riley telling me she hadn't kept her. And now this."

I consider my words for a few drawn out seconds, and then, "The really good thing is that she has you for a father. And she needs you to protect her. Riley could have killed you, Klein. I think you have to report it. Even if she isn't charged or punished, maybe it will stop her from doing something like this again."

"I know you're right. It's just so ugly."

"It is."

We're silent for a bit, and then he says, "Where are you?"

"I'm in Virginia. At my mom's house. She left me the place, and I haven't been here for a long time. Just kind of needed to get away."

"Ah. Are you and Josh—"

"No," I say. "We're not."

"Oh." There is relief in his voice. "Can I be honest, Dillon?"

"Yes."

"I miss you."

"I miss you, too."

"Will you give me some time to get my life straightened out?"

"Take all the time you need. I'll be here."

Klein

Fourteen months later

I'M SO NERVOUS, I can barely think.

Noelle and I walk among the early French paintings in my favorite section of the Louvre. I carry her with my right arm, answering her baby-talk questions with full answers because I mostly understand what she's asking when she points and babbles. I kiss her soft forehead, and she reaches a palm for my chin, grabbing and giggling.

"Okay, naughty Noelle," I tease, and she wriggles to my left arm, still laughing. The sound never fails to melt my heart.

I glance at my watch. She isn't late yet, so I don't know why I'm nearly sweating with nerves. I try to distract myself with more tutorials for Noelle, telling her who painted the enormous framed painting in front of us.

I feel her walk into the room before I ever turn around. I just know that she's there. Praying I'm right, I force myself to look, my heart thudding and thumping with all the elegance of a thirteen-year-old at his first dance. "Hey," I say, my eyes drinking her in.

"Hey," she says, shy as I've never heard her before.

I walk over to stand in front of her. "This is Noelle."

"Hi, Noelle," Dillon says, reaching out a hand to offer Noelle a finger to shake. Noelle does so with her chubby hand, and Dillon visibly melts.

We look at each other then, our eyes meeting, holding. I don't bother to hide how happy I am to see her, and if I'm right, she's just as happy to see me. "Thank you for coming," I say.

"Thank you for asking me."

"I wasn't sure you would."

"I wasn't sure I should. But here I am."

Suddenly, my plan feels clunky and not well-thought-out. What if I'm wrong? What if. . .I'm not going to let myself back out now. I reach for her hand, tug her gently across the room to the painting titled, *Trussing Hay*.

She looks at it and smiles. "I've thought of this painting so many times."

"So have I," I say. "And of our conversation about what it takes to create something lasting."

321

She looks up at me, nods, quiet, as if she knows I have something more to say. Noelle patty-cakes my cheek. I tickle her belly and say, "I'm pretty sure whatever art I've created isn't going to endure as long as what these artists created has. But there are two things in my life that I know will last. My love for this little girl. And my love for you, Dillon."

The surprise on her face is instant. Her voice breaks across my name. "Klein."

"Will you marry me, Dillon? Be our family?"

The tears slide down her face now, and I lean in to kiss her softly, with everything I feel for her completely evident. Noelle smooths a hand across Dillon's hair and coos.

Dillon is outright crying now, and she slips her arms around my neck, hugging Noelle and me both at the same time. "Yes," she says near my ear. "Yes, yes, yes."

We kiss again, but this time there's nothing tentative about it. It's hello, I've missed you, I want you, I need you. I feel complete, this circle of three we make, as if I will never need another thing to make me happy.

I pull back in a bit. "You have any opposition to getting married in Paris?"

"No opposition," she says, kissing me again. "No opposition at all."

Dillon

"I love you and that's the beginning and end of
everything."
—F. Scott Fitzgerald

AND THAT IS exactly what we do.

We elope, Klein, Noelle, and me in an afternoon
ceremony at the Chapelle Expiatoire, a beautiful old chapel
opened in 1826 and dedicated to King Louis XVI and
Marie Antoinette. It is late summer, and so the unheated
chapel is perfectly comfortable. I've had exactly a day to
find a dress, which really isn't that hard in Paris. Klein and
Noelle had gone with me to shop for it, and Noelle loved
it so much, we found her a tiny almost identical replica.

I carry a bouquet of white roses, and we are married
by an English-speaking French priest who treats our vows
with such sincerity that it is as if we are the first couple he
has ever married. Our kiss at the end is long and lingering,

and when Klein picks Noelle up, she kisses his cheek and then mine. My heart feels as if it will explode with happiness, and as we walk out of the chapel and into the city light, I feel as if I am walking into a wonderful new chapter of my life, everything that came before woven with good and not-so-good memories, but all of which have made me who I am today, a woman in love with and so very grateful for a new love with a man I adore, a man who loves me as I am.

~

KLEIN HAD BROUGHT a kind young nanny named Alyssa with them to Paris. She's from Signal Mountain, Tennessee, and she is wonderful with Noelle. But it is still hard to leave Noelle with her in their room across the hall. Klein has already put Noelle to bed though and tucked her in. She's fast asleep when we let ourselves out, Klein asking Alyssa to call us with any concerns at all. She assures us she will.

And so, when we step inside our suite, and he closes the door softly behind us, I feel as if I have stepped inside someone else's dream, that none of this can really be happening. Klein turns to face me, still dressed in his dark suit, the white shirt and tie striking against his incredibly handsome face. "Hello, wife."

I smile at this, just the word making my heart flutter. "Hello, husband."

Lamplight bathes the room in a soft glow. Klein reaches

for me, pulls me to him. And for some long, drawn-out moments, he simply holds me there against him. We look into each other's eyes, and words aren't really necessary. I see and feel what he is thinking, because it is what I am thinking, too. Life is not always easy to understand, the things that happen to us not even possible to explain, but then we arrive in safe harbor, and whatever ugliness has assailed us in the past, is no more. Something new and good has taken its place. "Mama was right," I say.

"How so?"

"You make my life bigger, better, greater."

Klein reaches a hand to my face, presses his palm to my cheek. And then he leans in to kiss me, our first alone as husband and wife, our first with the true freedom to give ourselves to each other fully. He grazes the backs of his hands across my shoulders, down my arms.

"You look so beautiful in this dress," he says. "Everything I never imagined having in a bride. You're beautiful, Dillon. And I am so grateful that you're mine."

I reach for him then, loosening his tie and undoing the first buttons of his shirt. He unzips the back of my dress, drops it to my waist. I feel no insecurity, no need to hide myself from him. I'm not perfect. I know this. And yet, it doesn't matter because I am loved. I know this, too.

"I love you, Klein. So much."

"I love you, baby," he says with a lingering kiss on my mouth. He reaches out to flick off the nearby lamp. And

then in the near dark, he lifts me into his arms and carries
me to bed.

Epilogue

From *Nashville News Today*, Nashville, Tennessee

Country Music Star and Songwriter Wife Start Home for Foster Kids

Country music superstar Klein Matthews and his award-winning songwriter wife, Dillon Blake-Matthews, have created and funded a new home for displaced foster kids, a safe place to land while waiting for a permanent placing. When asked what made the two of them get behind this project, Matthews says, "I grew up in the foster care system, and there are times when a child is between placements that it would be nice to have a home setting where a kid can just feel that he or she is wanted and safe. My wife, Dillon, has such a heart for these kids and made a video recently at the new place with the kids there singing her new hit song."

Known for writing heartrending country ballads that reflect life in small-town America, Blake-Matthews grew up as an only child but says, "I had so much love from my mother who pretty much devoted her life to helping me achieve my dreams. I can't imagine what it would be like to be a child alone in the world. If we can do anything to make a hurting child feel less lonely, I will feel like we've done something that matters."

Matthews married Dillon Blake, two-time recipient of the CMA Songwriter of the Year, in a secret Paris ceremony just over a year ago. Matthews's previous girlfriend and mother of his two-year-old daughter Noelle, Riley Haverson, was the subject of an investigation into allegations of a poisoning attempt on Matthews's life. Charges were dropped after an apparent mix-up at a testing lab where evidence in the case was mishandled. Haverson has since moved to Los Angeles, California. Matthews has full-custody of their daughter.

If You Enjoyed That Weekend in Paris. . .

Ren Sawyer and Lizzy Harper live completely different lives. He's a rock star with a secret he can no longer live with. She's a regular person whose husband stood her up for a long planned anniversary trip.

On a flight across the Atlantic headed for Italy, a drunken pity party and untimely turbulence literally drop Lizzy into Ren's lap. It is the last thing she can imagine ever happening to someone like her. But despite their surface differences, they discover an undeniable pull between them. A pull that leads them both to remember who they had once been before letting themselves be changed by a life they had each chosen.

Exploring the streets of Florence and the hills of Tuscany together – two people with seemingly nothing in common – changes them both forever. And what they find in each other is something that might just heal them both.

Buy it here.

That Birthday in Barbados

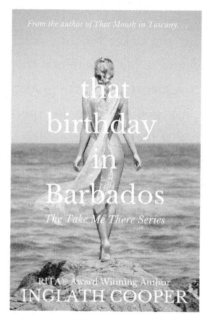

What is it about turning forty that makes a woman take a look at where she's been and make her wonder where she's going?

For ActivGirl CEO Catherine Camilleri, it is a crossroads that has her wondering where she went off

331

course. Divorced without children, life isn't what she had pictured for herself twenty years ago. Not up to admitting any of this in front of friends and family, she bails on the surprise party being thrown for her and books a last-minute trip to Barbados for a stay at the luxurious Sandy Lane Hotel, the same place where she'd spent her honeymoon ten years before. Is she going back to mourn the marriage she'd thought would last forever? Or in an attempt to chase out of her heart for good a betrayal that forever changed her?

Anders Walker might be just the ticket for that. After a brief career on Wall Street and a life experience that turned his world upside down, Anders took off the golden handcuffs and walked away for good. When he spots Catherine checking in on arrival at the Sandy Lane Hotel, he challenges her to try his spin class at the hotel's spa. He sees a woman who no longer considers herself someone a guy like him would be attracted to. Except that she's wrong. In Catherine, he recognizes a woman who defines herself by rejection. He sees, too, that she has made work her life. But he's learned that there is so much more to living. Simple things like swimming with sea turtles. And watching the sun sink on a Caribbean horizon. He's got two weeks to prove it to her, to make sure she will always remember that birthday in Barbados.

Buy it here.

Books by Inglath Cooper

That Weekend in Paris
That Birthday in Barbados
That Month in Tuscany
Swerve
The Heart That Breaks
My Italian Lover
Fences – Book Three – Smith Mountain Lake Series
Dragonfly Summer – Book Two – Smith Mountain
Lake Series
Blue Wide Sky – Book One – Smith Mountain Lake
Series
And Then You Loved Me
Down a Country Road
Good Guys Love Dogs
Truths and Roses
Nashville – Book Ten – Not Without You
Nashville – Book Nine – You, Me and a Palm Tree
Nashville – Book Eight – R U Serious

Nashville – Book Seven – Commit
Nashville – Book Six – Sweet Tea and Me
Nashville – Book Five – Amazed
Nashville – Book Four – Pleasure in the Rain
Nashville – Book Three – What We Feel
Nashville – Book Two – Hammer and a Song
Nashville – Book One – Ready to Reach
A Gift of Grace
RITA® Award Winner John Riley's Girl
A Woman With Secrets
Unfinished Business
A Woman Like Annie
The Lost Daughter of Pigeon Hollow
A Year and a Day

Dear Reader:

I would like to thank you for taking the time to read my story. There are so many wonderful books to choose from these days, and I am hugely appreciative that you chose mine.

Please join my mailing list for updates on new releases and giveaways! Just go to http://www.inglathcooper.com – come check out my Facebook page for postings on books, dogs and things that make life good!

Wishing you many, many happy afternoons of reading pleasure.

All best,

Inglath

About Inglath Cooper

RITA® Award-winning author Inglath Cooper was born in Virginia. She is a graduate of Virginia Tech with a degree in English. She fell in love with books as soon as she learned how to read. "My mom read to us before bed, and I think that's how I started to love stories. It was like a little mini-vacation we looked forward to every night before going to sleep. I think I eventually read most of the books in my elementary school library."

That love for books translated into a natural love for writing and a desire to create stories that other readers could get lost in, just as she had gotten lost in her favorite books. Her stories focus on the dynamics of relationships, those between a man and a woman, mother and daughter, sisters, friends. They most often take place in small Virginia towns very much like the one where she grew up and are peopled with characters who reflect those values and traditions.

"There's something about small-town life that's just part

of who I am. I've had the desire to live in other places, wondered what it would be like to be a true Manhattanite, but the thing I know I would miss is the familiarity of faces everywhere I go. There's a lot to be said for going in the grocery store and seeing ten people you know!"

Inglath Cooper is an avid supporter of companion animal rescue and is a volunteer and donor for the Franklin County Humane Society. She and her family have fostered many dogs and cats that have gone on to be adopted by other families. "The rewards are endless. It's an eye-opening moment to realize that what one person throws away can fill another person's life with love and joy."

Follow Inglath on Facebook

at www.facebook.com/inglathcooperbooks

Join her mailing list for news of new releases and giveaways at www.inglathcooper.com

Get in Touch With Inglath Cooper

Email: inglathcooper@gmail.com
Facebook – Inglath Cooper Books
Instagram – inglath.cooper.books
Pinterest – Inglath Cooper Books
Twitter – InglathCooper

Made in the USA
Monee, IL
06 August 2020

37707807R00204